LIVING A SUPERNATURAL, CHRIST-CENTERED LIFE

You Are Created In His Image And Likeness

Andre H. VanRooi

Kindle Publishing

CONTENTS

INTRODUCTION

As long as man has existed on this planet, there has been a hunger and desire for power outside the natural world, deep spirituality and the supernatural. Much of this inward desire have been translated into outward expressions of worship. This fact is evident in almost every part of the world. There are shrines, temples, statues, manmade gods all over this planet of ours, from Africa to Asia, the Himalayas to the Andes, and from the Atlantic to the Pacific oceans, that pay homage to some ancient or unknown deity. This is man's attempt to connect with the unseen world and make sense of our earthly existence.

We have always looked beyond the natural world because we have that even as beautiful and wonderful as it is, it does not satisfy our supernatural or spiritual hunger. This leads us to ask these questions: Why do we hunger for supernatural and spiritual things? Why do we have a 'built-in' desire for God or godlikeness? If life on this planet is all there really is, why are we searching as if we have lost something? Many have attempted, with the appearance of great authority and confidence, to answer this question, but their answers, theories and reasonings fall far short of answering the emptiness that exists in the human spirit. People who buy into these philosophies and theories, like I did, eventually realize the futility and emptiness of these belief systems. Is there an answer for mankind's dilemma, the sickness/darkness of our souls, the emptiness and meaninglessness of our lives?

These are questions which deserve honest answers. I believe that the Judeo-Christian Bible has the truth. Why do I believe that and why can I be so assured? I believe this and am so assured of it because I have studied many of these major philosophies and belief systems. Many people would lead you to believe that they are all the same but there are many fundamental differences in them. According to the definition of truth, there cannot be more than one truth, no matter how hard you try to reason and justify it. One of the fundamental differences is this statement Jesus made, when questioned about making the Father (God) known to man: Jesus answered, *"I am the way and the truth and the life. No one comes to the Father except through me. John 14:6 NIV.* Jesus claimed to be the only way for any human being to get to the Father (God). This one statement has been one of the most contentious claims Jesus made, other than being equal to God. For many years of my life, I did not accept this claim Jesus made, it was just too presumptuous.

Everything changed for me however, when I accepted Jesus' answer. I found that for those of us who fully accept, believe Jesus, and live the Judeo-Christian life, an incredible entrance into the supernatural world was opens up; one that we never knew existed. It is the only set of beliefs and writings that truly address the natural and spiritual origin of man. It is the only set of beliefs that delivers spiritual, physical, mental, and emotional healing. It is the only one that delivers hope, joy, peace, forgiveness of sins, and removes the fear of death from this life. It is the only one that truly reveals the nature of sin, and gives us power over it. It is the only one that exposes the ruler of darkness. It is the only one that offers an intimate relationship with a living God. No one has ever been able to disprove what's written, although many have tried, including me.

The Judeo-Christian Bible teaches us that human beings were created as supernatural (spiritual) beings who are meant to live supernatural lives. It actually teaches that we were created in the image and likeness of God, and therefore nothing but the spirit of the living God can give us spiritual life, purpose, or meaning. Since we are supernatural beings, nothing natural can satisfy this longing in our spirits (hearts) for the supernatural. Many human beings are very aware of the futility and meaninglessness of life, and as a result, many live in despair and hopelessness. This despair and hopelessness are evident in every nation, whether rich or poor, developed or undeveloped, educated or uneducated. It does not have to be that way. In this book, based on the Judeo-Christian Bible, I will address how we were created to live supernatural, godly lives.

JESUS SAID, YOU MUST BE BORN AGAIN

[3] Jesus answered and said to him, "Most assuredly, I say to you, unless one is born again, he cannot see the kingdom of God." John 3:3 NKJV

ANDRE H. VAN ROOI

The New Birth - Entrance To
The Supernatural World

For human beings to live a healthy supernatural/spiritual life, we need to be born again of the Spirit of the living God (the Father of Lights). There are many unhealthy spiritual practices, that do not lead to light or life, but instead lead to darkness and death. I have indulged in those unhealthy spiritual practices, and all they did was bring more darkness and confusion into my life. We do become like the God/gods we serve or worship; this is written in the Judeo-Christian Bible (Psalm 115:8).

The need to be born again of the Spirit of the Living God, was addressed by the Lord, Jesus Christ, early in His ministry when He was questioned by the religious leaders of His time. What is this need to be born again as expressed by the Lord? From the account below in the book of John, Nicodemus, a Jewish ruler and teacher, approaches Jesus and makes a statement about Jesus and His ministry. Jesus did not waste any time with Nicodemus and went directly to the heart of what Nicodemus really wanted to know and understand. Nicodemus had a desire to know, enter, and see the kingdom of God (the supernatural world that was beyond the physical world). He was aware of the lack of the supernatural in His life and their religious practices. There was no evidence of the kingdom of God that he knew was supposed to be available to them, in their religious practices and traditions. He knew the scriptures really well, and was aware of the reality of the spiritual world; but in his life and ministry, there appeared to be no manifestation of the spiritual, no matter how sincere he was in practicing his religion and their traditions. *He was spiritually bankrupt, but at least was aware of it. He saw the evidence of the supernatural in the life of Jesus, and knew that Jesus had something he did not have, and he desired it.*

[1] There was a man of the Pharisees named Nicodemus, a ruler of the Jews. [2] This man came to Jesus by night and said to Him, *"Rabbi, we know that You are a teacher come from God; for no one can do these signs that You do unless God is with him."* [3] *Jesus answered and said to him, "Most assuredly, I say to you, unless one is born again, he cannot see the kingdom of God."* [4] Nicodemus said to Him, "How can a man be born when he is old? Can he enter a second time into his mother's womb and be born?" [5] Jesus answered, *"Most assuredly, I say to you, unless one is born of water and the Spirit, he cannot enter the kingdom of God.* [6] *That which is born of the flesh is flesh, and that which is born of the Spirit is spirit.* [7] *Do not marvel that I said to you, 'You must be born again.'* [8] *The wind blows where it wishes, and you hear the sound of it, but cannot tell where it comes from and where it goes. So is everyone who is born of the Spirit."* John 3:1-8 NKJV

Why the need to be born again? Since Nicodemus already had life in the natural, it was apparent that Jesus was not talking about his natural existence. He said that *we need to be born of the Spirit of God again*; i.e *be born- again.* This means that mankind was once born of the Spirit of God, and then our spirit life experienced 'death'. The very first commandment God gave to man is recorded in the "Book of Beginnings" (Genesis). Since God made man, he had to give him instructions and directions on how to function in relationship with Him. The commandments God gave Adam were very simple. The one thing that was going to assure the life of Adam, was his obedience to the following directives God gave him:

[15] The Lord God took the man and put him in the Garden of

Eden to work it and take care of it. *16 And the Lord God commanded the man, "You are free to eat from any tree in the garden; 17 but you must not eat from the tree of the knowledge of good
and evil, for when you eat from it you will certainly die."* Genesis
2:15-17 NIV

The Fall (Spiritual Death) Of Man

This account of the spiritual death of man is recorded in the book of Genesis. Man's disobedience to God brought about the spiritual death of the first humans, and this death passed on to all their offsprings to this day.

¹ Now the serpent was more crafty than any of the wild animals the Lord God had made. He said to the woman, "Did God really say, 'You must not eat from any tree in the garden'?" ² The woman said to the serpent, "We may eat fruit from the trees in the garden, ³ but God did say, *'You must not eat fruit from the tree that is in the middle of the garden, and you must not touch it, or you will die.'"* ⁴ "You will not certainly die," the serpent said to the woman. ⁵ "For God knows that when you eat from it your eyes will be opened, and you will be like God, knowing good and evil." ⁶ When the woman saw that the fruit of the tree was good for food and pleasing to the eye, and also desirable for gaining wisdom, she took some and ate it. She also gave some to her husband, who was with her, and he ate it. ⁷ Then the eyes of both of them were opened, and they realized they were naked; so they sewed fig leaves together and made coverings for themselves. Genesis 3:1-7 NIV

We know that Adam and Eve did not die physically, because they lived for many more years after their spiritual death, and had many children. *This spiritual death meant a severed relationship and death of their spiritual life with God. It also caused mankind to lose their relationship, friendship, and companionship with the Holy Spirit. The Holy Spirit did not return to be with man, until Jesus left the planet.*

²¹ *The Lord God made garments of skin for Adam and his wife and*

clothed them. [22] And the Lord God said, "The man has now become like one of us, knowing good and evil. He must not be allowed to reach out his hand and take also from the tree of life and eat, and live forever." [23] So the Lord God banished him from the Garden of Eden to work the ground from which he had been taken. [24] After he drove the man out, he placed on the east side of the Garden of Eden cherubim and a flaming sword flashing back and forth to guard the way to the tree of life. Genesis 2:21-24 NIV

[1] *This is the written account of Adam's family line. When God created mankind, he made them in the likeness of God. [2] He created them male and female and blessed them. And he named them "Mankind" when they were created. [3] When Adam had lived 130 years, he had a son in his own likeness, in his* own image; and he named him Seth. [4] After Seth was born, Adam lived 800 years and had other sons and daughters. [5] *Altogether, Adam lived a total of 930 years, and then he died.* Genesis 5:1-4 NIV

The Life Of God And The Holy Spirit, Restored To Mankind Through Jesus

> *[16] For God so loved the world that He gave His only begotten Son, that whoever believes in Him should not perish but have everlasting life John 3:16 NIV*

It is because of His great love for His children, that God could not abandon them to a life of death and separation from Him, so He provided a Way for mankind to be restored back to Him. The way back to the Father is through Jesus Christ. I cannot say it any better than what has already been written in The Holy Bible, so let us look at what is written:

[9] Nicodemus answered and said to Him, "How can these things be?" [10] Jesus answered and said to him, "Are you the teacher of Israel, and do not know these things? [11] Most assuredly, I say to you, We speak what We know and testify what We have seen, and you do not receive Our witness. *[12] If I have told you earthly things and you do not believe, how will you believe if I tell you heavenly things?* [13] No one has ascended to heaven but He who came down from heaven, *that is,* the Son of Man who is in heaven. [14] And as Moses lifted up the serpent in the wilderness, even so must *the Son of Man be lifted up, [15] that whoever believes in Him should not perish but have eternal life. [16] For God so loved the world that He gave His only begotten Son, that whoever believes in Him should not perish but have everlasting life. [17] For God did not send His Son into the world to condemn the world, but that the world through Him might be saved.* [18] "He who believes in Him is not condemned; but he who does not believe is condemned already, because he has

not *believed in the name of the only begotten Son of God.* [19] And this is the condemnation, that the light has come into the world, and men loved darkness rather than light, because their deeds were evil. [20] For everyone practicing evil hates the light and does not come to the light, lest his deeds should be exposed. [21] But he who does the truth comes to the light, that his deeds may be clearly seen, that they have been done in the sight of God. John 3:9-21 NIV

"I am the way and the truth and the life. No one comes to the Father except through me. John 4:16 NIV

[22] Since you have purified your souls in obeying the truth through the Spirit in sincere love of the brethren, love one another fervently with a pure heart, [23] *having been born again, not of corruptible seed but incorruptible, through the word of God which lives and abides forever,* 1 Peter 1:22-23 NKJV

These truths recorded for us in the Bible cannot be understood by our natural minds. I remember trying to make sense of God, Jesus Christ, The Holy Spirit, and the Bible, before I was born again of the Spirit of the Living God. It was a difficult task, because the natural mind cannot comprehend spiritual things, without the spirit of man being given new life. Once the veil is lifted from our spiritual eyes, then we are able to start seeing the things of the spirit, that have been hidden from our view. *The restoration of our spiritual lives is our entrance into the kingdom of the son of His love (Collossians 1:13) and opens up 'new' realms of the spiritual world to us, realms that we were completely ignorant of because our minds were blinded by the god of this world (2 Corinthians 4:4).*

The life and death of Jesus Christ ushered in a new dispensation for mankind, into the world of the supernatural/spiritual. Jesus came to expose the works of darkness that blinded the hearts and minds of mankind. Once he exposed the works of darkness (sin, sickness, disease, pain, demonic possession, etc.) and people saw it, they clamored to be delivered and set free from them.

We will look at the purpose and the role of The Holy Spirit of God in depth more in a later chapter, but for now, take note that the precious Holy Spirit was sent back to the world, as a gift to us, after Jesus' departure from the earth.

"But I tell you the truth, it is to your advantage that I go away; for if I do not go away, the Helper will not come to you; but if I go, I will send Him to you. John 16:7 NASB

How Do I Become Born Again?

If you declare with your mouth, "Jesus is Lord," and believe in your heart that God raised him from the dead, you will be saved. Romans 10:9 NIV

God made it so simple and accessible, that even a little child can understand and receive the new life God has made available to us. As Paul stated in the book to the Roman church, you must say out of your mouth: *"Jesus you are Lord, and I believe in my heart that God raised You from the dead. Amen."* Yes, it is that simple. The adventure of a lifetime into the supernatural begins for us, after we are born again of the Spirit of God.

SEEK AFTER HIM (KNOWING GOD)

¹² Then you will call upon Me and go and pray to Me, and I will listen to you. ¹³ And you will seek Me and find Me, when you search for Me with all your heart. ¹⁴ I will be found by you, says the Lord, Jeremiah 29:12-14a NIV

After our new life in Jesus Christ begins and our lost relationship with the Father is restored, we have to continue our journey into the supernatural. Anything important to us; which we treasure and are passionate about, are things that we seek after (diligently work at or pursue); good or bad. We devote resources (time, money, energy, etc.) and sometimes spare no cost in these endeavors. One thing I have learned over the years is that there is no greater treasure to pursue after than God. His kingdom and righteousness are the pearls of great price (Matthew 13:44-46), that every man should pursue after. All other pursuits leave us empty and exasperated, because only that which is truly of God's spirit, can satisfy our spirits. Throughout His Word, God implores us to seek Him, not because He needs us, but because He knows what will bring us the most joy and fulfillment. He made us after all and knows what we need to be complete, not lacking anything.

²³ Thus says the Lord: "Let not the wise man glory in his wisdom, Let not the mighty man glory in his might, Nor let the rich man glory in his riches; **24** But *let him who glories glory in this, that he understands and knows Me*, That I am *the Lord, exercising lovingkindness, judgment, and righteousness* in the earth. For in these I delight," says the Lord. Jeremiah 9:23-25 NKJV

12 Then you will call upon Me and go and pray to Me, and I will listen to you. 13 And you will seek Me and find Me, when you search for Me with all your heart. 14 I will be found by you, says the Lord, Jeremiah 29:12-14a NKJV

but *the people who know their God* shall be strong, and carry out great exploits. Daniel 11:32b NKJV

The Consistent Message

The message of God to His people remains consistent throughout His Word. Jesus and the apostles declared the same message spoken by the prophets who went before them: *Seek God, because He wants to be found by us, and reveal Himself to us.* There are many wonderful and supernatural things for us to discover (seek after), inside the kingdom of God. *We should have a childlike wonder and fascination about God and His kingdom.* Jesus said that unless we receive the kingdom of God like a little child; curios and excited about it, we will not be able to enter into it (Luke 18:17)

Truly I tell you, *anyone who will not receive the kingdom of God like a little child will never enter it.*" Mark 10:15 NIV

[33] *But seek first his kingdom and his righteousness*, and all these things will be given to you as well. Matthew 6:33 NIV

[6] But without faith *it is* impossible to please *him*: for he that cometh to God must believe that he is, and *that he is a rewarder of them that diligently seek him*. Hebrews 11:6 KJV

Seeking after God, will take us down many wonderful, but oftentimes, challenging paths. The rewards however, are truly supernatural and exhilarating. We will devote the remainder of this book, exploring the path God gave us to seek after Him.

KNOWING JESUS AS LORD, MASTER, KING AND GOD.

[15]The Son is the image of the invisible God, the firstborn over all creation.
Colossians 1:15 BSB

T o fully understand the Bible and the supernatural world, we have to understand who Jesus really is. This understanding puts in perspective what Jesus taught and demonstrated during His life on earth. It is this understanding of who He is, that gives us a revelation of who we really are. We step into the supernatural by allowing Him to express Himself through us.

[16]For in Him all things were created, things in heaven and on earth, visible and invisible, whether thrones or dominions or rulers or authorities. *All things were created through Him and for Him. [17]He is before all things, and in Him all things hold together.*[18]And He is the head of the body, the church; He is the beginning and firstborn from among the dead, so that in all things He may have preeminence.[19]*For God was pleased to have all His fullness dwell in Him,[20] and through Him to reconcile to Himself all things, whether things on earth or things in*

heaven, by making peace through the blood of His cross. Colossians 1:16-20 BSB

Most of the Christian world sees Jesus as our Savior; the one who redeemed us from our sin and made a way for us to get to heaven. Most of the non-Christian world see Him as a prophet, a good man, a fake, and/or the founder of a religion. However, The Word tells us He is much more than a Savior or the founder of a religion.

The disciples and others used several titles to address Jesus. The most common titles they used were: *Lord, Master, and King.* They even addressed Him as their God. These titles or references were not ceremonial, like so many of those in the religious world had, but instead, they spoke of who He is; His power and authority that He exerts in the spiritual and natural world (kingdom). Jesus did not stop them from referring to Him in this way, because that is who He truly is.

We understand dominion, power, and authority in the natural world, but sometimes we do not understand it in the spiritual. We have seen from history, and experienced the rule, reign and destruction of earthly kingdoms/governments. We have seen power shift from one group/party to another and with that often comes new ways of doing things because of the implementation of new laws, rules and regulations. Sometimes these changes of government/rule bring about great freedom and joy to its citizens, but oftentimes it brings death, destruction, poverty, confusion, etc.

The fall of man caused the ruler of darkness (Satan) to become the god of the kingdoms of this world: spiritual, political, economic, educational, social, media and entertainment, etc. With the rule and reign of this king of darkness, came spiritual darkness, death, destruction, sickness, disease, poverty and all kind of evil and wickedness; as mankind forgot who they were really created to be. *We were translated from the kingdom of light, into the kingdom of darkness.*

Therefore, just as *sin entered the world through one man, and death through sin*, and in this way death came to all people, because all sinned—Romans 5:12 NIV

³But even if our gospel is veiled, it is veiled to those who are perishing, *whose minds the god of this age has blinded*, who do not believe, lest the light of the gospel of the glory of Christ, who is the image of God, should shine on them. 2 Corinthians 4:3-4 NKJV

Satan ruled and reigned in the kingdoms of this world with very little opposition or challenge, until Jesus came to re-take this authority from him, and began to establish the kingdom of heaven here on earth. Jesus, the greater King; through His obedience and suffering, overcame/defeated the devil and rescued us from the devil's kingdom/rule making us citizens/members of His kingdom. *He translated us from the kingdom of darkness back to the kingdom of light.*

¹⁸ And Jesus came and spoke to them, saying, *"All authority has been given to Me in heaven and on earth.* ¹⁹ Go therefore and make disciples of all the nations, baptizing them in the name of the Father and of the Son and of the Holy Spirit *Matthew 28:18-19 NKJV*

¹³ *He has delivered us from the power of darkness* and *conveyed us into the kingdom of the Son of His love Colossians 1:13 NKJV*

He who sins is of the devil, for the devil has sinned from the beginning. *For this purpose the Son of God was manifested, that He might destroy the works of the devil. 1 John 3:8 NKJV*

But you are a *chosen people*, a *royal priesthood*, a *holy nation*, God's special possession, that you may declare the praises of him who called you out of darkness into his wonderful light. *1 Peter 2:9 NIV*

As priests and kings of His kingdom He delegated His power and authority to us, and backs it up with the armies and the power of heaven.

> [*The Twelve Apostles*] And when He had called His twelve disciples to Him, *He gave them power over unclean spirits, to cast them out, and to heal all kinds of sickness and all kinds of disease.* Matthew 10:1 NKJV

> [Sending Out the Twelve] Then He called His twelve disciples together and *gave them power and authority over all demons, and to cure diseases.* Luke 9:1 NKJV

> Behold, *I give you the authority to trample on serpents and scorpions, and over all the power of the enemy*, and nothing shall by any means hurt you. Luke 10:19 NKJV

Jesus has power to give life and to destroy it (Matthew 10:28). He is the creator of everything and rules over all of creation (John 1:1-10). God placed Jesus far above all principalities, power, might, dominion, and every name that is named, not only in this world, but also in the world that is to come: *And he put all things under his feet (authority), and gave him to be the head over all things to the church*, which is his body, the fulness of him that fills all in all. (Ephesians 1:21-22 KJV). He had the power/authority to summons legions of angels to come and protect Him (Matthew 26:53), but he restrained himself in order to fulfill the will of God.

Despite His power and authority, He does not dictate to us how we should live our lives, follow or obey Him. We must all *willingly*, *humbly*, and *reverently* submit ourselves to His *Lordship*, *rule*, and *authority*. He provides clear instructions to us; in His Word, on what He expects/requires from us (as we will explore later), but He never forces us to obey His Word. *Every wise child of God will make it their highest duty to find out from God's Word what He requires from them, and will pursue Him with the greatest passion and diligence.*

We should pray like Paul did in Ephesians 1:17-19: *[17] That the God of our Lord Jesus Christ, the Father of glory, may give unto you (us) the spirit of wisdom and revelation in the knowledge of him: [18] The eyes of your (our) understanding being enlightened; that ye (we) may know what is the hope of his calling, and what the riches of the glory of his inheritance in the saints, [19] And what is the exceeding greatness of his power to us-ward who believe, according to the working of his mighty power,*

Jesus As Lord And Master

The word Lord/Master, from the Helps Word studies is defined as *a person exercising absolute ownership rights*. When we refer to Jesus as our Lord/Master, we are inferring that He rules over everything and owns everything in our lives. Since most of us in democratic, western societies have never lived under Lords or Masters (the closest we have gotten is landlord). Sometimes we cannot completely relate to or understand this concept. However, it is important for us to learn and understand the true nature and character of Jesus, not only to view Him as our Savior, brother and friend; but to understand His position of power and authority in our lives and over all of creation (seen and unseen).

Jesus As Lord

This is he who was spoken of through the prophet Isaiah: "A voice of one calling in the wilderness, '*Prepare the way for the Lord*, make straight paths for him.'" Matthew 3:3 NIV

Peter said to Jesus, "*Lord, it is good for us to be here. If you wish, I will put up three shelters, one for you, one for Moses and one for Elijah.*" Matthew 17:4 NIV

Jesus did not let him, but said, "*Go home to your own people and tell them how much the Lord has done for you*, and how he has had mercy on you." Mark 5:19 NIV

And he will go on before the Lord, in the spirit and power of Elijah, to turn the hearts of the parents to their children and the disobedient to the wisdom of the righteous—*to make ready a people prepared for the Lord.*" Luke 1:17 NIV

Today in the town of David a Savior has been born to you; *he is the Messiah, the Lord.* Luke 2:11 NIV

Jesus As Master

When I studied Buddhism and practiced Kung Fu, I had a master/teacher ('sifu' in Cantonese). My greatest goal and desire was to learn as much as I could from my master and if at all possible, become like him (skilled in the art of Kung Fu). At our 'sifu's' command, we would subject ourselves to extreme physical duress and pain, in order to gain mastery over our bodies, our will, and our minds. Under my master's tutelage, I became very skilled in the art of empty-handed combat, fighting with weapons, and mastering different fighting styles, developed by the Buddhist monks.

When I accepted Jesus as my Savior, I learned that His disciples knew Him as their Master. This was an easy concept for me to understand, since I already knew what it meant to be subject to a master. Under my new Master however, I had to re-learn how to gain mastery over my body, will and mind, in a completely different way, for very different reasons. I began to learn, that the ways of my new Master were completely different from the ways of my old masters (Satan and my Kung Fu teacher).

Simon answered, "*Master*, we've worked hard all night and haven't caught anything. But because you say so, I will let down the nets." Luke 5:5 NIV

The disciples went and woke him, saying, "*Master, Master*, we're going to drown!" He got up and rebuked the wind and the raging waters; the storm subsided, and all was calm. Luke 8:24 NIV

Remember what I told you: 'A servant is not greater than his *master*.' If they persecuted me, they will persecute you also. If they obeyed my teaching, they will obey yours also. John 15:20 NIV

It is our duty as disciples of Jesus Christ to not only learn the ways of our master, but to yield our lives, willingly, to His will and His ways. We should not be guilty of the statement Jesus made to His first set of disciples: *"Why do you call me, 'Lord, Lord,' and do not do what I say? (Luke 6:46 NIV)*. It is in this place of obedience and yielded-ness, that we learn to enter into the supernatural, the way He intends for us. *It was, and still is His desire that His disciples become like their Master.*

Jesus As King

The nation of Israel had many kings who ruled over them, but through their disobedience and sin, their kingdom was eventually destroyed, and the rule of kings of Israel and Judah came to an end. They were living under Roman government and rule at the time Jesus was revealed to them. The Jewish people, once again, were looking for a deliverer, to free them from the oppressive rule of another non-Jewish state/rule. Since king David was considered their greatest and most powerful king, they were hoping that Jesus would be a king like David. Jesus is indeed a king, but not the kind of king that His people were looking for, and His kingdom was definitely not from this world: Jesus answered, *"My Kingdom is not an earthly kingdom. If it were, my followers would fight to keep me from being handed over to the Jewish leaders. But my Kingdom is not of this world."* John 18:36 NLT. He was recognized by the prophets of old, not only as the king of Israel, but also as the king of all the kingdoms of this world and all nations.

"Where is the one who has been born *king* of the Jews? We saw his star when it rose and have come to worship him Matthew 2:2 NIV

"Say to Daughter Zion, 'See, your *king* comes to you, gentle and riding on a donkey, and on a colt, the foal of a donkey.'" Matthew 21:5 NIV

"Are you the *king* of the Jews?" asked Pilate. "You have said so," Jesus replied. Mark 15:2 NIV

"Blessed is the *king* who comes in the name of the Lord!" "Peace in heaven and glory in the highest!" Luke 19:38 NIV

Then Nathanael declared, "Rabbi, you are the Son of God; you are the *king* of Israel." John 1:49 NIV

They took palm branches and went out to meet him, shouting, "Hosanna!" "Blessed is he who comes in the name of the

Lord!" "Blessed is the *king* of Israel!" John 12:13 NIV

and sang the song of God's servant Moses and of the Lamb: "Great and marvelous are your deeds, Lord God Almighty. Just and true are your ways, *King of the nations*. Revelation 15:3 NIV

We must recognize Him as the King who He is, but I think we often fail in doing this. I see often in the church at large, how we act overfamiliar with Him, like He is our childhood friend. We should ask The Father to give us a revelation of who Jesus really is, and what His stature is in heaven and in all of creation. When we learn and understand the place Jesus occupies in eternity, we will better understand what we have access to in the supernatural and natural worlds.

Jesus As God

Throughout The Holy Bible, Jesus is also referred to as God. This description of Jesus is the one that many people and religions have major issues with. They have no problem seeing Jesus as a prophet, good teacher, great miracle worker, etc. But God? That is way too presumptuous and downright blasphemous. *He does not fit into their picture of God, as if somehow their perception of Him carries greater weight and more importance than who He really is.* The fact that He was God in the flesh, is called out to us by the prophets of old and not so old. It was also demonstrated by Jesus Himself, throughout His life on earth.

All right then, the Lord himself will give you the sign. Look! The virgin will conceive a child! *She will give birth to a son and will call him Immanuel (which means 'God is with us')*. Isaiah 7:14 NLT

For to us a child is born, to us a son is given, and the government will be on his shoulders. And he will be called Wonderful Counselor, *Mighty God, Everlasting Father*, Prince of Peace. Isaiah 9:6 NIV

Satan, who is the god of this world, has blinded the minds of those who do not believe. They are unable to see the glorious light of the Good News. *They don't understand this message about the glory of Christ, who is the exact likeness of God.* 2 Cor 4:4 NLT

Though *he was God*, he did not think of equality with God as something to cling to. Phil 2:6 NLT

I do not know about you, but the fact that Jesus was God in the flesh is absolutely thrilling and amazing. It speaks to me of a God who has made Himself available and approachable to us. This speaks of His great love for His creation, so much so, that He never stopped desiring that we would know Him, be close to Him, and be restored to the original intent and purpose He had for us.

There are many things we will not fully understand until we see Jesus with unveiled eyes. This revelation of Him as God is one of those things. However we do have His Word, Works, and The Holy Spirit to reveal and bear witness of the truth. He is Immanuel; God with us and in us. Knowing and relating to Him as Lord, Master, King, and God makes the supernatural more natural for us, so we do not view it as an occasional experience we have (only during 'revival' services; or special meetings), but as part of the riches of our glorious inheritance in God's Holy people.

THE SUPREME IMPORTANCE OF GOD'S WORD

When it comes to partaking of the supernatural, the importance of God's Word cannot be over emphasized. We cannot separate God from His Word, they are one. Through His Word, His nature and character are revealed to the world. His Word also reveals His intent and purpose for all things. His Word reveals the mysteries that mankind wrestle with, as we try to make sense of the world. His Word gives the solution to all the problems that plague mankind. His Word is the life force that sustains everything in our universe, and beyond. His Word reveals to us, the supernatural things that were once hidden from our view.

His Word Will Remain Forever And Will Never Fail

Every Word that God has spoken will come to pass. This should cause us to pause and consider the words God has spoken, because many of these words pertain to our very lives and our eternal destiny. God is bound by His word and there is nothing greater than His word. It is written for us to know that, He esteems His Word above His own name (*Psalm 138:2*)

⁸ *For my thoughts are not your thoughts*, neither are your ways my ways, saith the Lord. ⁹ For as the heavens are higher than the earth, so are my ways higher than your ways, and my thoughts than your thoughts. ¹⁰ For as the rain cometh down, and the snow from heaven, and returneth not thither, but watereth the earth, and maketh it bring forth and bud, that it may give seed to the sower, and bread to the eater: ¹¹ *So shall my word be that goeth forth out of my mouth: it shall not return unto me void, but it shall accomplish that which I please, and it shall prosper in the thing whereto I sent it.* Isaiah 55:8-11 NKJV

Heaven and earth will pass away, but my *words will never pass away.* Matthew 24:35 NIV

¹⁶ "The law and the prophets *were* until John. Since that time the kingdom of God has been preached, and everyone is pressing into it.¹⁷ *And it is easier for heaven and earth to pass away than for one tittle of the law to fail.* Luke 16:16-17 NKJV

These truths about The Word of God should give us great confidence, assurance and boldness in the fact and reality of the supernatural world. I, however, have met many 'believers' who have a shaky confidence in God's Word, and therefore in God Himself. *Their human reasoning casts long shadows of doubt over the truth and veracity of the Word of God.* As a result, I have seen them stumble around in darkness, never entering into the incredible supernatural things made available to us. Many of them were once taught others, but somewhere along the way, they lost sight of the truth and power that is in God's Word. *I have also seen others who have decided to implicitly believe God's Word, even if they do not fully understand everything in it. They have decided that since He is their God, they will enter fully into the supernatural life He made available to them. For them, God watches over His Word, and performs it.*

Jesus Christ: The Word Of God Revealed.

Since God is so holy and lives in unapproachable light, He reduced himself to become like us in order to grant us access to Him. God never desired for His children to be separated from Him, however sin caused us to lose our relationship with Him. It is through Jesus, that God became approachable and relatable to mankind. God was showing us, through Jesus, who we were created to be. *Since Jesus was the first born amongst many (Romans 8:29), He is the blueprint for the rest of us, who were born again as a result of His death and resurrection.*

> *[1] In the beginning was the Word, and the Word was with God, and the Word was God. [2] He was with God in the beginning. [3] Through him all things were made; without him nothing was made that has been made.*[4] In him was life, and that life was the light of all mankind. John 1:1-4 NIV

> *[14] The Word became flesh and made His dwelling among us.* We have seen His glory, the glory of the one and only Son from the Father, full of grace and truth. John 1:14 BSB

> *[8]Philip said to Him, "Lord, show us the Father, and that will be enough for us." [9]Jesus replied, "Philip, I have been with you all this time, and still you do not know Me? Anyone who has seen Me has seen the Father. How can you say, 'Show us the Father'? [10]Do you not believe that I am in the Father and the Father is in Me? The words I say to you, I do not speak on My own. Instead, it is the Father dwelling in Me, performing His works. [11]Believe Me that I am in the Father and the Father is in Me—or at least believe on account of the works themselves. John 14:8-11 BSB*

Not only did Jesus give us access to the Father, who is the ultimate Spirit, but He opened up the way for us to enter the supernatural spirit world, where God rules and reigns. Jesus showed us in so many different ways, what living a supernatural life is all about. He even told us that this world was made available to us (we will take a look at this later).

His Word Keeps Everything Together

I spent almost a decade of my life studying Buddhism, dabbled in the occult and believed in other 'supernatural' things, like aliens, crop circles, space ships, parallel universes, etc. I also believed in evolution as the source of all life on our planet. *I was one of many seekers, and we were always looking for something beyond the natural world we found ourselves in.* The Word of God seemed silly and unintelligent to us because we thought ourselves to be more intelligent and enlightened than the simple-minded people, who believed God's Word. How close-minded/hearted, ignorant, and oftentimes, arrogant we were. *The Word of God is the ultimate revelation of the supernatural. Not only did it open my spiritual eyes to the things unseen, but it gave me access to this unseen world, which God 'hid' in plain sight for those who are humble enough to receive Him.*

God has spoken and revealed Himself to mankind, in various ways during our existence on planet earth. His final word to mankind, however, was His son, Jesus Christ. Since then He has not spoken anything more to us. There is no greater revelation the Father can give us, than His only begotten son:

[1] In the past God spoke to our ancestors through the prophets at many times and in various ways, [2] but *in these last days he has spoken to us by his Son*, whom he appointed heir of all things, and through whom also he made the universe. [3] The Son is the radiance of God's glory and the exact representation of his being, *sustaining all things by his powerful word.* After he had provided purification for sins, he sat down at the right hand of the Majesty in heaven. Hebrews 1:1-3 (NIV)

God made the universe through His Son that He sustains all things through Him. I must admit, that this concept has been a little difficult for me to grasp because my finite mind is so limited and He is so unlimited in how He thinks and does things. His majesty and omnipotence humble me; and to think I thought I knew it all.

Our Responsibility Towards
God's Word

Hide God's Word In Your Heart – Study, Meditate On It, Obey It

God gave Joshua very specific instructions, after he assumed the leadership role over Israel. Moses, his predecessor, could not enter the land of God's promise to His people, but was laid to rest outside the borders of it. Moses was a fearless and resolute leader and is still revered by the Jewish people today, as their great prophet. God worked mightily through Moses to deliver the children of Israel (Abraham) as he led them for forty years in the desert. Anyone taking over from Mose had some mighty big shoes to fill. However, whoever took over from Moses, had the same God on their side, and the same hosts of heaven willing and able to assist when they took over. The instructions for living in and attaining the supernatural was no different for Joshua, than it was for Moses, and it is no different for us as modern-day children of God. Let us look at the instructions God gave to Joshua:

[1] After the death of Moses the servant of the Lord, it came to pass that the Lord spoke to Joshua the son of Nun, Moses' assistant, saying: [2] "Moses My servant is dead. Now therefore, arise, go over this Jordan, you and all this people, to the land which I am giving to them—the children of Israel. [3] Every place that the sole of your foot will tread upon I have given you, as I said to Moses. [4] From the wilderness and this Lebanon as far as the great river, the River Euphrates, all the land of the Hittites, and to the Great Sea toward the going down of the sun, shall be your territory. [5] *No man shall be able to*

stand before you all the days of your life; as I was with Moses, so I will be with you. I will not leave you nor forsake you. ⁶ Be strong and of good courage, for to this people you shall divide as an inheritance the land which I swore to their fathers to give them. ⁷ Only be strong and very courageous, that you may observe to do according to all the law which Moses My servant commanded you; do not turn from it to the right hand or to the left, that you may prosper wherever you go. ⁸ This Book of the Law shall not depart from your mouth, but you shall meditate in it day and night, that you may observe to do according to all that is written in it. For then you will make your way prosperous, and then you will have good success. ⁹ Have I not commanded you? Be strong and of good courage; do not be afraid, nor be dismayed, for the Lord your God is with you wherever you go." Joshua 1:1-9 (NKJV)

God could not make His promises and instructions any clearer to Joshua! In between His incredible promises to Joshua, He sandwiched instructions about Joshua's responsibility toward His Word. The three responsibilities Joshua had were:

- **Obey** God's Word (be careful to observe to do it)
- **Speak** God's Word (do not let it depart from your mouth)
- **Become intimately familiar** with God's Word (study it, and meditate on it day and night)

It is interesting to take a note of Joshua's life and experiences with God during Moses' life. Whenever Moses was called to meet with God one on one, Joshua , his servant, would always go along. Joshua experienced the power and the presence of God throughout his life. When Moses was called up to the mountain to meet with God, Joshua went along. When Moses met with God in the tent of meeting outside the camp, Joshua was there. It was during these meetings that God would talk to Moses and give Him instructions and direction for the great task at hand. When Moses left the tent, Joshua always remained behind in the glory and presence of God.

> [7]Now Moses used to take the tent and pitch it at a distance outside the camp. He called it the Tent of Meeting, and anyone inquiring of the LORD would go to the Tent of Meeting outside the camp. [8]Then, whenever Moses went out to the tent, all the people would stand at the entrances to their own tents and watch Moses until he entered the tent. [9]As Moses entered the tent, the pillar of cloud would come down and remain at the entrance, and the LORD would speak with Moses. [10]When all the people saw the pillar of cloud standing at the entrance to the tent, they would stand up and worship, each one at the entrance to his own tent. *[11]Thus the LORD would speak to Moses face to face, as a man speaks to his friend. Then Moses would return to the camp, but his young assistant Joshua son of Nun would not leave the tent.* Exodus 33:7-11 BSB

It is interesting to note that God did not even mention any of Joshua encounters as requirements for a successful and prosperous life; as wonderful as they probably were. *God put all the emphasis of His instructions to Joshua, on his responsibility towards His Word.* Let us be wise builders of our lives and not the foolish ones; whom Jesus talked about, as we will look at, in the next section. We must build our lives on God's Word.

Build Your Life Upon His Word – Put It To Practice.

It is no surprise that the theme of the criticality of God's Word from Genesis to Malachi continues from Matthew to Revelation. Jesus reiterated these truths and painted a powerful picture of the need for us to not only hear His Word, but also put them it practice.

*24 "Therefore everyone who hears these words of mine and puts them into practice is like a wise man who built his house on the rock. 25 The rain came down, the streams rose, and the winds blew and beat against that house; yet it did not fall, because it had its foundation on the rock.*26 But everyone who hears these words of mine and does not put them into practice is like a foolish man who built his house on sand. 27 The rain came down, the streams rose, and the winds blew and beat against that house, and it fell with a great crash." Matthew 7:24-27 NIV

*22But prove yourselves doers of the word, and not merely hearers who delude themselves.*23For if anyone is a hearer of the word and not a doer, he is like a man who looks at his natural face in a mirror;*24for once he has looked at himself and gone away, he has immediately forgotten what kind of person he was.*25But one who looks intently at the perfect law, the law of liberty, and abides by it, not having become a forgetful hearer but an effectual doer, this man will be blessed in what he does. James 1:22-25 NASB*

It is hard for me to understand why anyone would read these instructions in God's Word and not pay much attention to or follow them. The results of ignoring them are so detrimental, yet many choose to go their own way, like the first man; Adam. Obeying God's Word brings life; disobeying it brings destruction and ultimately death.

The books of Psalms and Proverbs are filled with the importance and the power of knowing, obeying and meditating on God's Word.

9 How can a young man cleanse his way? By taking heed according to Your word.

10 With my whole heart I have sought You; Oh, let me not wan-

der from Your commandments!

¹¹ *Your word I have hidden in my heart, That I might not sin against You.*

¹² Blessed *are* You, O Lord! Teach me Your statutes.

¹³ With my lips I have declared All the judgments of Your mouth.

¹⁴ I have *rejoiced* in the way of Your testimonies, As *much as* in all riches.

¹⁵ I will *meditate on* Your precepts, And contemplate Your ways.

¹⁶ I will *delight myself in* Your statutes; *I will not forget Your word.* Psalm 119:9-16 NKJV

¹ Hear, my children, the instruction of a father, And give attention to know understanding;

² For I give you good doctrine: Do not forsake my law.

³ When I was my father's son, Tender and the only one in the sight of my mother,

⁴ He also taught me, and said to me: *"Let your heart retain my words; Keep my commands, and live.*

⁵ Get wisdom! Get understanding! Do not forget, nor turn away from the words of my mouth.

⁶ Do not forsake her, and she will preserve you; Love her, and she will keep you.

⁷ Wisdom is the principal thing; Therefore get wisdom. And in all your getting, get understanding.

⁸ Exalt her, and she will promote you; She will bring you honor, when you embrace her.

⁹ She will place on your head an ornament of grace; A crown of glory she will deliver to you."

¹⁰ Hear, my son, and *receive my sayings, And the years of your life will be many.*

[11] I have taught you in the way of wisdom; I have led you in right paths.

[12] When you walk, your steps will not be hindered, And when you run, you will not stumble.

[13] *Take firm hold of instruction, do not let go; Keep her, for she is your life.*

[20] *My son, give attention to my words; Incline your ear to my sayings.*

[21] *Do not let them depart from your eyes; Keep them in the midst of your heart;*

[22] *For they are life to those who find them, And health to all their flesh.* Proverbs 4 NKJV.

We live in an age in time where all the temporal things around us change rapidly. We have made swift advances in technology, medicine and just about every industry. As a result, we seem to believe that somehow God's Word and His ways have become outdated and obsolete. In our lives we are reaping the results of these mindsets and attitudes, which prove that our systems of thought and philosophies have failed us all. Results such as broken hearts, lives, families, communities, cities, nations and a broken world. God has always been true, but every man who does not agree with God, a liar. Do not take my word for it, look at the world around you, and prove it out in your own life. I have certainly found God and His Word to be true. *Only a foolish person (which I was at one time), would take God and His Word lightly.*

Let His Word Always Be On Your Lips

Throughout the Holy Bible, we are reminded and encouraged to speak and profess God's Word. *His Words are spirit and life, and He watches over His Word to perform it. Speaking God's Word builds your faith, because faith comes by hearing, and hearing by the Word of God.* When God hears His Word spoken by His children, in faith, He confirms His Word with signs and wonders.

[20] "The Redeemer will come to Zion, to those in Jacob who repent of their sins," declares the Lord. [21] "As for me, this is my covenant with them," says the Lord. "My Spirit, who is on you, will not depart from you, and *my words that I have put in your mouth will always be on your lips, on the lips of your children and on the lips of their descendants—from this time on and forever*," says the Lord. Isaiah 59:20-21 NIV

And the disciples went everywhere and preached, and *the Lord worked through them, confirming what they said by many miraculous signs*. Mark 16:20 NLT

The easiest way to do this, if you have not spoken out God's Word on a regular basis, is to start in Psalms. Read them out loud with passion and emotion. Try to picture yourself as the writer of the Psalm, and imagine what He was feeling when he wrote it. If it seems unnatural to you at first, keep going, it will eventually become natural to you. As you speak God's Word, you will build up your own spirit man and your faith in God will actually begin to grow and increase *(So then faith comes by hearing, and hearing by the word of God. Romans 10:17 NKJV)*. Faith goes beyond our natural senses, and awakens the life of our spirit. *Faith takes you from the natural world, into the supernatural world*. Why is this important? Because God communes with our spirits *(For his Spirit joins with our spirit to affirm that we are God's children Romans 8:16 NLT)*.

Study To Show Yourself Approved

In the beginning of our journey in Christ, we should read and become familiar with the Word of God. However, if you have been on the journey for a while, it is not enough anymore to merely read God's Word, and be familiar with it. A deeper level of commitment and understanding of the Word is required. You only achieve this by studying God's Word; line upon line, precept upon precept.

> *Study to shew thyself approved unto God*, a workman that nee-
> deth not to be ashamed, rightly dividing the word of truth. 2
> Timothy 2:15 KJV

The way I started deepening my level of commitment to God's Word, was to write His Word down; book by book and line by line. I went through all the books from Matthew to Revelation this way. I was amazed at all I found. Things I did not see before, through only reading through the Bible. I know now why God commanded the kings of Israel to write for themselves a copy of the law, it forces you to pay attention to His Word. Once you have mastered this task, then you can do a topical study; e.g. Study the Holy Spirit, the Kingdom of God, Healing, Fruits and Gifts of the Spirit, etc. and see how a theme unfolds around these topics. At this stage you have become a student of God's Word. There is a boldness and confidence that will come upon you, as the Word of God saturates your heart and soul.

HONOR GOD (JESUS) AND OBEY HIS WORD

L et us dig a little deeper into our responsibility, as it relates to obeying God's Word, as a pre-requisite for living a supernatural life. The matter of honoring God is of extreme importance to Him, because to obey or disobey, is often a matter of life or death for us (as evidenced by Adam and Eve, Moses, King Saul, Ananias and Saphira). Obedience to God means that we honor and respect (highly esteem) Him. God says that He will honor those who honor Him. Honoring God is being obedient to His Word. When God brought the children (descendants) of Israel (Abraham) out of Egypt, He desired to establish them as a holy nation, set apart for Him. He desired for them to reflect His nature and character, so that they could give evidence of His existence. He desired to reveal Himself to the other nations through them, so that He could fulfil the promise He made to Abraham:

[15] Then the Angel of the Lord called to Abraham a second time out of heaven, [16] and said: "By Myself I have sworn, says the Lord, because you have done this thing, and have not withheld your son, your only *son*— [17] blessing I will bless you, and multiplying I will multiply your descendants as the stars of the heaven and as the sand which *is* on the seashore; and your descendants shall possess the gate of their enemies. *[18] In your seed all the nations of the earth shall be blessed, because you have obeyed My voice."* Genesis 22:15-18 NKJV

After they were set free from slavery in Egypt, God took the time to give them the blueprint for a successful life on this planet by teaching them how to live a life that was pleasing to Him. This blueprint (God's Word) was given to Moses, who recorded everything God told Him for the nation of Israel (read Deuteronomy 30).

According to God, the opposite of honoring Him is to despise Him. 1 Samuel 2:30 NKJV [30]Why the LORD God of Israel said, I said indeed that your house, and the house of your father, should walk before me for ever: but now the LORD said, *Be it far from me; for them that honor me I will honor, and they that despise me shall be lightly esteemed.*

The following instructions from Jesus about obedience to God's Word, bear repeating:

[46] *"But why do you call Me 'Lord, Lord,' and not do the things which I say?* [47] *Whoever comes to Me, and hears My sayings and does them, I will show you whom he is like:* [48] *He is like a man building a house, who dug deep and laid the foundation on the rock. And when the flood arose, the stream beat vehemently against that house, and could not shake it, for it was founded on the rock.* [49] But he who heard and did nothing is like a man who built a house on the earth without a foundation, against which the stream beat vehemently; and immediately it fell. And the ruin of that house was great." Luke 6:46-49 NKJV

It should be obvious to us by now (if we have been paying attention), is that God has made it very clear what He requires of us. *However, what God commands, we often view as optional. Obedience to God, often comes down to us making the decision to serve and follow Him.* Honoring and obeying God brings us life and only adds to us. God still desires to reveal Himself to the world, through His children. Honoring God and obeying His Word, gives us legitimate access to the Godly supernatural world, that exists in Him.

As For Me And My House, We Will Serve The Lord

Throughout our lives we will all be challenged and confronted by the tendency to live in our flesh, as the Bible puts it. Not only are we challenged by our own flesh, but the flesh of others, especially those closest to us. It is during these times, that we are presented with the choice of who we really want to serve. Do we serve our flesh, do we comprise and serve the god of this world, or do we serve the Lord?

Joshua as the new leader of Israel, had to deal with the flesh of others, in servitude to the Lord. From his statement below, we see that there were many in Israel who no longer desired to serve the Lord, or who were double-minded about their commitment to the God; who so mightily delivered them from Egypt. Joshua confronted them about their double-mindedness and hesitancy to fully commit their lives to the Lord:

> [15] *And if it seems evil to you to serve the Lord, choose for yourselves this day whom you will serve*, whether the gods which your fathers served that were on the other side of the River, or the gods of the Amorites, in whose land you dwell. *But as for me and my house, we will serve the Lord."* Joshua 24:15 NKJV

The other gods, Joshua was referring to, are still among us today. They did not die or leave the planet yet. They lust after the spirits and bodies of man, and they go to great lengths to get us to serve and worship them. *When we are confronted by their enticing ways, we are all left with the choice; whether to serve them, or serve the one we call, Lord.*

To Obey Is Better Than Sacrifice

The people of Israel desired a king to rule over them like the other nations around them. God desired to be their king, but they chose to have a man rule over them. A man named Saul was chosen from among them to rule. *Like all men, he had many shortcomings, but his greatest weakness was his reluctance or inability to obey the Word of the Lord.* God instructed Saul to destroy the Amalekites as punishment for what they did to Israel on their way out of Egypt. God told him to kill all the men, women, children, and infants, oxen, sheep, camels and donkeys. Saul partly obeys the Lord's command by killing all the people but he spares the king. He kills almost all of the livestock, but keeps the best of them for himself and his men. This act of disobedience angers God so much, that He expresses His regret to Samuel for making Saul king. Samuel understands the gravity of Saul's disobedience and he cries out to God all night, probably for mercy in His judgement. Saul is so impressed with himself that he goes to erect a monument of himself, to celebrate his victory.

When Samuel finally catches up with Saul, and confronts him about his disobedience, Saul's response was that his men kept all the best cattle to sacrifice to the Lord. Samuel's response to Saul should be a warning to us all. Let us look at his response:

> So Samuel said: *"Has the Lord as great delight in burnt offerings and sacrifices, As in obeying the voice of the Lord? Behold, to obey is better than sacrifice, And to heed than the fat of rams.* [23]For rebellion is as the sin of witchcraft, And stubbornness is as iniquity and idolatry. *Because you have rejected the word of the Lord, He also has rejected you from being king."* [24]Then Saul said to Samuel, "I have sinned, for I have transgressed the commandment of the Lord and your words, because I feared the people and obeyed their voice. 1 Samuel 15:22-23 NKJV

Saul's disobedience brought three things to light in his life: He was a rebel against God, he was stubborn and he rejected God's Word (he feared people more than he feared God). As king of Israel, his act of disobedience would infect an entire nation, if left unpunished. God equates Saul's rebellion to witchcraft and his stubbornness as idolatry. The rest of Saul's life is a sad decline into jealousy, rage and insanity. God rejects him to select and prepare David to become king of Israel. Saul loses his throne, his sons and eventually his own life, in subsequent battles against David and his men. These are the devastating results of disobedience to God's instructions, in our lives. *Obedience to God's commands would have brought Saul and his descendants, a lifetime of natural and supernatural rewards; but instead, his disobedience brought destruction and death.*

Take Up The Cross And Follow Him

Jesus issued this challenge to His first disciples and it flies into the face of most of His modern-day followers. We love the benefits of being a disciple or follower of His, but the denying of ourselves for His sake, is a hard pill to swallow. Jesus loves us, but He will never go easy on us because He desires the best for us.

24 Then Jesus said to His disciples, *"If anyone desires to come after Me, let him deny himself, and take up his cross, and follow Me.* 25 For *whoever desires to save his life will lose it, but whoever loses his life for My sake will find it.* 26 For what profit is it to a man if he gains the whole world, and loses his own soul? Or what will a man give in exchange for his soul? 27 *For the Son of Man will come in the glory of His Father with His angels, and then He will reward each according to his works.* 28 Assuredly, I say to you, there are some standing here who shall not taste death till they see the Son of Man coming in His kingdom." Luke 9:24-28 NKJV

Could this be one of the main reasons few people enter into the supernatural world Jesus came to reveal to us. Is it because we are not willing to pay the price? The price for our salvation was certainly not cheap, yet He took up His cross in order to see us enter into the life the Father had originally created for us. *His challenge still stands, 2020 years later: If you desire to come after Me, deny yourself, take up your cross and follow me.* It is a tall order, but it is a path we all must take as true follower of Jesus Christ.

Who Jesus Considers Family

In my lifetime of serving the Lord, I have heard and sung many songs that talks about me being a friend of God, Jesus being my brother, and me, being a part of God's family. There is truth in these statements, of course, but they are not without condition. I have observed others, and I myself, have lived at times like God has no standards or requirements. We do not want to condemn God's children for their weaknesses and failures, however, *a culture of cheap grace has swept through the church, taking away the responsibility every believer has to order their lives after God's principles.* No one was spared the 'wrath' of Jesus in this matter, not even His own mother and brothers.

46 While He was still talking to the multitudes, behold, His mother and brothers stood outside, seeking to speak with Him. **47** Then one said to Him, "Look, Your mother and Your brothers are standing outside, seeking to speak with You." **48** But He answered and said to the one who told Him, "Who is My mother and who are My brothers?" **49** And He stretched out His hand toward His disciples and said, *"Here are My mother and My brothers!* **50** *For whoever does the will of My Father in heaven is My brother and sister and mother."* Matthew 12:46-50 KJV

My fellow believers, there is no cheap grace and there are no shortcuts to a life that is pleasing and approved by God. Do not be deceived by men and women who profess to be speaking for God, but teach things that are contrary to God's Word. Read God's Word for yourself, asking the Holy Spirit to teach, lead, and guide you into all truth. *Discover what the will of God is. It is revealed in His Word, through His Holy Spirt.* Your eternal destiny depends on it.

Be Strong In Grace And Be Diligent To Show Yourself Approved Of God

The apostle Paul instructed Timothy in no uncertain terms, of the importance of presenting himself as being approved by God, not men. It is by rightly dividing the Word of truth so that God's approval is obtained and causes one not to be ashamed. The grace that is in Christ Jesus, gives us the strength to live a life that is pleasing to God and to obtain His approval.

[1]You then, my son, be strong in the grace that is in Christ Jesus. [2]And the things you have heard me say in the presence of many witnesses entrust to reliable people who will also be qualified to teach others. [3]Join with me in suffering, like a good soldier of Christ Jesus. [4]No one serving as a soldier gets entangled in civilian affairs, but rather tries to please his commanding officer. [5]Similarly, anyone who competes as an athlete does not receive the victor's crown except by competing according to the rules. [6]The hardworking farmer should be the first to receive a share of the crops. [7]Reflect on what I am saying, for the Lord will give you insight into all this.

[8]Remember Jesus Christ, raised from the dead, descended from David. This is my gospel, [9]for which I am suffering even to the point of being chained like a criminal. But God's word is not chained. [10]Therefore I endure everything for the sake of the elect, that they too may obtain the salvation that is in Christ Jesus, with eternal glory. [11]Here is a trustworthy saying: If we died with him, we will also live with him; [12]if we endure, we will also reign with him.

If we disown him, he will also disown us; [13]if we are faithless, he remains faithful, for he cannot disown himself. [14]Keep reminding God's people of these things. Warn them before God against quarreling about words; it is of no value, and only ruins those who listen. [15]Do your best to present yourself to God as one approved, a worker who does not need to be ashamed and who correctly handles the word of truth. [16]Avoid godless chatter, because those who indulge in it will become more and more ungodly. [17]Their teaching will spread like gangrene. Among them are Hymenaeus and Philetus, [18]who have departed from the truth. They say that the resurrection has already taken place, and they destroy the faith of some. [19]Nevertheless, God's solid foundation stands firm, sealed with this inscription: "The Lord knows those who are his," and, "Everyone who confesses the name of the Lord must turn away from wickedness."[20]In a large house there are articles not only of gold and silver, but also of wood and clay; some are for special purposes and some for common use. [21]Those who cleanse themselves from the latter will be instruments for special purposes, made holy, useful to the Master and prepared to do any good work. [22]Flee the evil desires of youth and pursue righteousness, faith, love and peace, along with those who call on the Lord out of a pure heart. [23]Don't have anything to do with foolish and stupid arguments, because you know they produce quarrels. [24]And the Lord's servant must not be quarrelsome but must be kind to everyone, able to teach, not resentful. [25]Opponents must be gently instructed, in the hope that God will grant them repentance leading them to a knowledge of the truth, [26]and that they will come to their senses and escape from the trap of the devil, who has taken them captive to do his will. 2 Timothy 2 NIV

This entire section of the letter Paul wrote to Timothy, clearly captures the principles of a life that is pleasing to and approved by God. We are instructed, together with Timothy, by our older brother. Paul lived this life and eagerly passed on his life experience and revelations to this young disciple of Jesus Christ, and pupil of his. I wonder how many of us actually pause to ask God the question: *Do you approve of my life Father? Is it pleasing to you?*

The grace in the Lord, is what makes us pleasing to God. We can absolutely live a life that God approves, because He has given us everything that pertains to live and godliness (2 Peter 1:3).

Being Like The Master

Every discipline and art form in the world has masters (teachers), student and disciples. Students often became masters after many decades of study and the application of what they have learnted. Masters often look for students to whom they can entrust their art, skill, wisdom and secrets (*Matt 13:10-12, Luke 8:10 So He said, "The secrets of the kingdom of God have been given for you to know, but to the rest it is in parables, so that Looking they may not see, and hearing they may not understand.*).

Once they have selected these students, the master would pour His heart and life into them. Quite often, these students are put through strenuous challenges to test their knowledge, commitment (faithfulness) and skill. They need to prove that they are worthy of the master's time and energy and that they can be trusted with the master's secrets. Not all students who are chosen, make it all the way to the level of the master. Many bow out along the way or do not make the cut, but for the few who make it, the rewards are tremendous.

Jesus was a master and teacher (one could say a master teacher). He had many things to teach His selected/chosen students (disciples). One of the key things His disciples had to learn was that if they were going to be like Him, they would have to do what He did, and endure what He endured. *It all seems simple and easy when we say the prayer of salvation and ask Jesus into our hearts to be our Lord and our Savior. It is an entirely different story to be devoted and committed to the Master, giving our lives completely over to Him, to allow Him to conform us into His image (Romans 8:29).* Ask the apostle Peter. Ask the many believers who face persecution, on a regular basis, for their belief in Jesus Christ. Ask yourself the question, do I have what it takes to truly follow Jesus and devote my life to Him. Do not be that quick to say 'yes' like Peter, and then when the time of your testing comes, deny the Lord.

Jesus gave ample warning about what was ahead to those who wished to become His disciples. There were thousands of people who followed Jesus around wherever He went during His earthly ministry. There were, however, very few who actually became His disciples. It is the same today. Many profess to be followers of the Lord, but very few are willing to become disciples. What is the difference between a disciple and a follower? A disciple will endure what his master endures and will follow him to the end. *Followers will only go as long as it is comfortable, but when times of testing come, they are the first ones to bail out (John 6:66, Matthew 26:56).*

[24] *"A disciple is not above his teacher, nor a servant above his master.* [25] *It is enough for a disciple that he be like his teacher, and a servant like his master.* If they have called the master of the house Beelzebub, how much more will they call those of his household! [26] Therefore do not fear them. For there is nothing covered that will not be revealed, and hidden that will not be known. Matthew 10:24 NKJV

[40] *A disciple is not above his teacher, but everyone who is perfectly trained will be like his teacher.* Luke 6:40 NKJV

[18] "If the world hates you, you know that it hated Me before it hated you. [19] If you were of the world, the world would love its own. Yet because you are not of the world, but I chose you out of the world, therefore the world hates you. [20] *Remember the word that I said to you, 'A servant is not greater than his master.'* If they persecuted Me, they will also persecute you. If they kept My word, they will keep yours also. [21] *But all these things they will do to you for My name's sake, because they do not know Him who sent Me.* John 15:18-21 NKJV

[7] During the days of Jesus' life on earth, *he offered up prayers and petitions with fervent cries and tears* to the one who could save him from death, and *he was heard because of his rever-*

ent submission. [8] Son though he was, he learned obedience from what he suffered [9] and, once made perfect, he became the source of eternal salvation for all who obey him Hebrews 5:7-9 (NIV)

To enter and remain in the supernatural world Jesus opened up for us, requires becoming like Him. To share in the power of His resurrection, we must share in the fellowship of His suffering. These are high and lofty goals and aspirations, but are attainable. The Lord desires that we enter His world, so that we can see things we have never seen before and do things we have never done before.

Be Holy (Set Apart)

The importance of holiness cannot be emphasized enough, but is often completely overlooked and under taught in the modern church. It is not given the emphasis it requires. Yet, it is also foundational to our faith and a relationship with a holy God. We often shy away from this topic because we might consider it difficult to obtain or too 'religious'. Other times when it is taught, it often takes on a condemning tone and is used to 'beat' up the people. Holiness often takes on a certain persona, that presents itself as something that is displayed outward, such as a certain way of dressing, wearing your hair, an absence of things that might be considered too 'worldly,' like jewelry or makeup, etc. When we review the meaning of holy, it gives us an idea of what God's intention was for calling us to live a holy life.

HELPS Word-studies : 40 *hágios* – properly, *different* (*unlike*), *other* ("*otherness*"), *holy*; for the believer, 40 (*hágios*) means "*likeness of nature with the Lord*" because "*different* from the world."

The fundamental (core) meaning of 40 (*hágios*) is "different" – thus a temple in the 1st century was *hagios* ("holy") because *different* from other buildings (Wm. Barclay). In the NT, 40 / *hágios* ("holy") has the "technical" meaning "*different from the world*" because "*like the Lord.*"

[40 (*hágios*) implies something "set apart" and therefore "*different (distinguished/distinct)*" – i.e. "other," *because special to the Lord.*]

What is evident from God's Word, is His instruction (requirement) for us to be holy. If we examine the impact/results of holiness (being set apart for God Himself), it becomes clear that it is something of great benefit to those who pursue it. *Not only does our holiness give evidence/witness to the fact that God is true and real, it is actually very attractive when done the right way.* Holiness will also keep you spiritually, physically, mentally, and emotionally healthy. The bottom line is, holiness is very good for you.

Since God never changes, His requirements of His people, do not change. Throughout the history of God's dealing with His people, He called them out to be different from the world and othe nations around them.

> "For you are a holy people to the Lord your God; the Lord your God has chosen you to be a people for Himself, a special treasure above all the peoples on the face of the earth. Deuteronomy 7:6 NKJV

> For you are a holy people to the Lord your God, and the Lord has chosen you to be a people for Himself, a special treasure above all the peoples who are on the face of the earth. Deuteronomy 14:2 NKJV

> But you are a chosen generation, a royal priesthood, a holy nation, His own special people, that you may proclaim the praises of Him who called you out of darkness into His marvelous light; 1 Peter 2:9 NKJV

> [3] Blessed be the God and Father of our Lord Jesus Christ, who has blessed us with every spiritual blessing in the heavenly places in Christ, [4] just as He chose us in Him before the foundation of the world, that we should be holy and without blame before Him in love, [5] having predestined us to adoption as sons by Jesus Christ to Himself, according to the good pleasure of His will, Ephesians 1:3-5 NKJV

> that He might present her to Himself a glorious church, not having spot or wrinkle or any such thing, but that she should be holy and without blemish. Ephesians 5:27 NKJV

> but as He who called you is holy, you also be holy in all your conduct, because it is written, "Be holy, for I am holy." 1 Peter 1:15-16 NKJV

He who is unjust, let him be unjust still; he who is filthy, let him be filthy still; he who is righteous, let him be righteous still; *he who is holy, let him be holy still.*" Revelation 22:11 NKJV

It often comes down to a choice for us to live a holy life. The bottom line is, we must choose life over death and it is a choice we must make on a regular basis. We must pursue it with passion and intensity. We will often stumble along the way and make mistakes, but as long as we keep it as a focus of our lives, we will, through the help of the Holy Spirit, attain greater measures of holiness in our lives. We will live a supernatural life which will become a normal part of our daily lives.

THE MATTER OF LOVE: ACCEPTING AND LIVING IT

We know how much God loves us, and we have put our trust in his love. God is love, and all who live in love live in God, and God lives in them 1 John 4:16 NLT

I do not think that it would be too far-fetched to say that love holds the universe together, and makes it function the way it is supposed to. God is love and He holds the universe together and makes it function. Admittedly, love is one of the many attributes of God, but it is His primary motivation for saving a lost world. Love is also one of the primary elements that opens up the world of the supernatural to us. The entire Bible can be viewed as a love story, with God, Jesus and the Holy Spirit, as the main characters. Then, there is the villain, Satan, who not only tried to usurp God's authority and rule in heaven; but also came to kill, steal and destroy the very creation of God: man. Then, there is mankind, desperately needing to be rescued from sin and the rule of Satan over our lives, which we so easily surrendered through disobedience to God's commands. *God's love for man compelled Him to make the greatest sacrifice ever made in history; to sacrifice His one and only begotten Son, purchasing our salvation, with the blood of Jesus.*

Accept God's Unconditional Love

¹⁶ For God so loved the world that He gave His only begotten Son, that whoever believes in Him should not perish but have everlasting life. John 3:16 NKJV

Since we were created by a God who is love (1 John 4:8b), *we were created to love and be loved unconditionally.* I will say that a little differently, *we were created to give love and receive love unconditionally. Unconditional love, is one of the most important ingredients for our successful development as human beings.* When we are not unconditionally loved, or experience conditional love as children, it creates many emotional problems in our lives. We take these problems into our future (marriage, family, work, finances etc.) It makes us vulnerable to abuse and exploitation.

Where do we start? *We start by accepting the fact that God unconditionally loves us.* He did not only say He loves us, but He proved it by offering Jesus for us. Not only does He love us unconditionally, but He also does not condemn us when we believe in Him.

¹⁷ For God did not send His Son into the world to condemn the world, but that the world through Him might be saved. ¹⁸ *"He who believes in Him is not condemned;* John 3:17-18b NKJV

⁶ For when we were still without strength, in due time *Christ died for the ungodly.* ⁷ For scarcely for a righteous man will one die; yet perhaps for a good man someone would even dare to die. *⁸ But God demonstrates His own love toward us, in that while we were still sinners, Christ died for us.* ⁹ Much more then, having now been justified by His blood, we shall be saved from wrath through Him. *¹⁰ For if when we were enemies we were reconciled to God through the death of His Son, much*

more, having been reconciled, we shall be saved by His life. [11] And not only that, but we also rejoice in God through our Lord Jesus Christ, through whom we have now received the reconciliation. Romans 5:6-11 NKJV

It can be hard to accept that there is someone who loves us as much as God does, but it is one of the most beautiful truths and realities of the Gospel of our Lord and Savior, Jesus Christ. This is part of the unseen world we were given access to by our Lord. The world we never knew existed or experienced in our lives before Him. It might take you some time to get used to this idea of being loved unconditionally, by our heavenly Father, but it is a liberating truth. W*e do deserve to be loved that way. He is the perfect and ultimate Father, one many of us never had.* Love helps us blossom and grow. It makes us healthy and whole human beings.

You might need to remind yourself, every once and a while, that God really, really, loves you.

Love God

You shall love the Lord your God with all your heart, with all your soul, and with all your strength. Deuteronomy 6:5 NKJV

Every command and directive God has given to man greatly benefits us and is necessary for us to function properly. This is important to understand: He made us so He knows exactly what we require to be whole (holy). *When God, therefore, commands us to love Him, it is not because He is in need of our love, but it is what makes us function as we were designed.* There is tremendous power in the expression of genuine love. Love has the power to transform and heal broken lives, bodies and minds (I go into great detail on the transformation of our minds in my book: *Extreme Mind Makeover: The God Edition*).

Science and psychology have made tremendous progress in understanding the power of love and the impact of it on our lives. God, in His Word, tells us to incline our ears (listen) to His saying (Word), because it is life to those who find it and strength to all their flesh. He has repeatedly told us to trust Him and obey Him. *These directives to walk in His ways and love Him have been the most important ones He has given us.*

[*The Essence of the Law*] "And now, Israel, what does the Lord your God require of you, but to fear the Lord your God, to *walk in all His ways* and to *love Him*, to *serve the Lord your God with all your heart* and with all your soul: Deuteronomy 10:12 NKJV

Love Yourself.

[19]We love because He first loved us 1 John 4:20 NKJV

On my faith journey I have found that too many of God's children, do not love themselves. God is love and when we love, even ourselves, we reflect His nature and character. *When we love ourselves, we love what He loves.* Often the most overlooked part of the greatest commandment Jesus taught us, is the fact that *we should love ourselves.* [37]*Jesus said to him, "'You shall love the Lord your God with all your heart, with all your soul, and with all your mind.' [38]This is the first and great commandment. [39]And the second is like it: 'You shall love your neighbor as yourself.' [40]On these two commandments hang all the Law and the Prophets." Matthew 22:37-40 NKJV*

Some of you may disagree with me making this inference from what Jesus said, but you would be assuming that all of us love ourselves (and, therefore, will love our neighbor as we love ourselves). *The reason we often struggle to love others, is because we have a difficult time loving ourselves.* I believe that we should love ourselves because God loves us and considers us valuable (precious). It is not a strange thing that God the Father would love His children. He is the perfect Father and we do not have to earn His love. His love is not conditional (*Psalm 103 – Praise For The Lord's Mercies*). Why do you think so much emphasis was given to the Father's love for us in His Word? It is because we have to be reminded, over and over again, of His unconditional love for us. It is said that when a person hears one negative thing said about them in a hurtful way, they need to be told something positive 100 times, to offset that one negative thing. Do you now understand why the Father throughout His Word, keeps letting us know that He loves us and cares about us?

What do you think? If a man owns a hundred sheep, and one

of them wanders away, will he not leave the ninety-nine on the hills and go to look for the one that wandered off? And if he finds it, truly I tell you, he is happier about that one sheep than about the ninety-nine that did not wander off. In the same way, *your Father in heaven is not willing that any of these little ones should perish.* Matthew 18:12-14 NKJV

The Spirit you received does not make you slaves, so that you live in fear again; rather, the Spirit you received brought about your adoption to sonship And by him we cry, "Abba, Father." *The Spirit himself testifies with our spirit that we are God's children.* Romans 8:15-16 NKJV

[18] knowing that *you were* not *redeemed* with corruptible things, like silver or gold, from your aimless conduct received by tradition from your fathers, [19] but *with the precious blood of Christ,* as of a lamb without blemish and without spot. 1 Peter 1:18-20 NKJV

See what great love the Father has lavished on us, that we should be called children of God! And that is what we are! 1 John 3:1 NKJV

Love Your Neighbor (Others)

You shall not take vengeance, nor bear any grudge against the children of your people, but you shall love your neighbor as yourself: I am the Lord. Leviticus 19:18 NKJV

Once we have learned to accept God's love, love Him and love ourselves, we are now in a better position to love our neighbor, which includes our brothers and sisters in the Lord. This command however, is probably the one in which you will be tested the most, and on a regular basis. It is only in this testing, that the hidden things of our hearts are exposed. When we learn to excel in this area, we begin to exhibit the nature and the character of the God who created us. I am not saying you will become gods, but rather that you will reflect Him more, to a world that is seeking and are hungry for the kind of love that only comes from God: *And this hope will not lead to disappointment. For we know how dearly God loves us, because he has given us the Holy Spirit to fill our hearts with his love. Romans 5:5 NLT.* God is making His love available to us through the Holy Spirit. This should give us the assurance that we can fulfil this great commandment given to us.

I will repeat this statement: *God did not leave us guessing about what He requires of us.* He made His requiremetns abundantly clear through His spokesmen, throughout the ages,instructing us how live an abundant, blessed and supernatural life.

[34] But when the Pharisees heard that He had silenced the Sadducees, they gathered together. [35] Then one of them, a lawyer, asked Him a question, testing Him, and saying, [36] "Teacher, which *is* the great commandment in the law?" [37] Jesus said to him, *"'You shall love the Lord your God with all your heart, with all your soul, and with all your mind.'* [38] This is the first and great commandment. [39] And the second *is* like it:

'You shall love your neighbor as yourself.' [40] On these two commandments hang all the Law and the Prophets." Matthew 22:34-40 NKJV

By this all people will know that you are my disciples, *if you have love for one another.*" John 13:35 ESV

For the commandments, "You shall not commit adultery," "You shall not murder," "You shall not steal," "You shall not bear false witness," "You shall not covet," and if there *is* any other commandment, *are all summed up in this saying, namely,* "You shall *love your neighbor as yourself.*" Romans 13:9 NKJV

For all the law is fulfilled in one word, even in this: "You shall *love your neighbor* as *yourself.*" Galatians 5:14 NKJV

If you really fulfill the royal law according to the Scripture, "You shall *love your neighbor as yourself,*" you do well; James 2:8 NKJV

[7] *Beloved, let us love one another, for love is of God; and everyone who loves is born of God and knows God.* [8] He who does not love does not know God, for God is love. [9] In this the love of God was manifested toward us, that God has sent His only begotten Son into the world, that we might live through Him. [10] In this is love, not that we loved God, but that He loved us and sent His Son to be the propitiation for our sins. [11] *Beloved, if God so loved us, we also ought to love one another.* 1 John 4:7-11 NKJV

Our marching orders have been made very clear by our commander and chief, the Lord Jesus Christ. He, Himself, demonstrated love even to those who denied, mocked, cursed and crucified Him (the apostle Paul, being one of the most wellknown amongs them). Remember, a disciple is not above his master. A true disciple will deny himself the rights and privileges he once held dear, and humble himself in obedience to his master.

You might have heard it said, that love is a verb, meaning it is something that we do, instead of something we feel. *Love is an outward expression of an inward conviction*. The apostle beautifully summed up for us how love works or are expressed in a few sentences. Based on his description of what love does, we can determine if we are really loving our neighbor.

> [4] *Love suffers long and is kind; love does not envy; love does not parade itself, is not puffed up;* [5] *does not behave rudely, does not seek its own, is not provoked, thinks no evil;* [6] *does not rejoice in iniquity, but rejoices in the truth;* [7] *bears all things, believes all things, hopes all things, endures all things.* [8] *Love never fails. 1 Corinthians 13:4-8 NKJV*

I like how this instruction to us by the Holy Spirit concludes: *Love never fails*. I like to think of it this way, love never gives up and it always sees victory in every trial or situation we encounter. *Love is the fuel for the engine of our soul that keeps it going, when we would rather give up.*

Based on the description of what love does, it begs the questions: how do you measure up? w*hat is your love IQ?* We can all definitely grow in this area and every other area of our lives, through the help of the Holy Spirit. Let us discover and learn how we can grow in this area, in the next chapter.

THE HOLY SPIRIT – SUPERNATURAL HUMAN EMPOWERMENT

The Holy Spirit is often referred to as the third person of the Trinity (God Head); the Trinity being the Father, Son and Holy Spirit. The precious Holy Spirit is not an "it" or the '"anointing", as we often refer to Him. *The Holy Spirit is as much God, in the same manner as the Father and the Son.* Most of us in the church-world are more familiar and comfortable with the Father and the Son, but we often lack understanding of the relevance, importance, role and purpose of The Holy Spirit.

The church was in the heart (loins) of the Father, built upon Jesus (He is the foundation), and given birth to by The Holy Spirit. The Book of Acts is the book of the working (acts) of the Holy Spirit. He birthed and equips the church, working mightily and powerfully through it. The Holy Spirit is the key to the life and success of the church. *The same power that started the church, is required to sustain it and to give it life and vitality.* Much of what we consider the church today, is not even a shadow of what The Lord intended it to be. In general, this is due to our disobedience to His

ANDRE H. VAN ROOI

Word, and the general absence of The Holy Spirit in the life of the modern church. We tend to focus more on our buildings, agendas and programs, rather than His mission and purpose for His called-out ones.

The Lord gave much emphasis to the importance and the work of The Holy Spirit. The Lord, Himself, was baptized by The Holy Spirit when He was baptized by John the Baptist in the Jordan river. He started and continued His earthly ministry, empowered by The Holy Spirit.

¹³ Then Jesus came from Galilee to John at the Jordan to be baptized by him. ¹⁴ And John tried to prevent Him, saying, "I need to be baptized by You, and are You coming to me?" ¹⁵ But Jesus answered and said to him, "Permit it to be so now, for thus it is fitting for us to fulfill all righteousness." Then he allowed Him. ¹⁶ *When He had been baptized, Jesus came up immediately from the water; and behold, the heavens were opened to Him, and He saw the Spirit of God descending like a dove and alighting upon Him.* ¹⁷ And suddenly a voice came from heaven, saying, "This is My beloved Son, in whom I am well pleased." Matthew 3:13-17 NKJV

³⁷ that word you know, which was proclaimed throughout all Judea, and began from Galilee after the baptism which John preached: ³⁸ *how God anointed Jesus of Nazareth with the Holy Spirit and with power, who went about doing good and healing all who were oppressed by the devil, for God was with Him.* ³⁹ And we are witnesses of all things which He did both in the land of the Jews and in Jerusalem, whom they killed by hanging on a tree. Acts 10:37-39 NKJV

It is vital for us to know and understand the importance of The Holy Spirit in the life of every believer, and, therefore the church. *God said that it is not by might or power but by His spirit (Zechariah 4:6), that His will/work would be accomplished and completed on the earth.* Jesus was physically limited in His earthly body, as well as in His heavenly body. He could only be in one place at a time. Even today, Jesus is seated in heaven and does not come to earth much (people have reported Jesus appearing to them here on earth, like He did to the disciples after His resurrection, but there are no reports of Jesus appearing in different places at the same time, even in His glorified (resurrected) body). *The same power that raised Jesus from the dead, now lives inside of us, to make us like Him* (which is God's ultimate intent and purpose for His children), but Jesus, Himself, is not omnipresent.

The Holy Spirit is not limited in this way. He is working all over the earth, at the same time, in the life and heart of every human who welcome Him. Jesus said the Holy Spirit would be our *helper, teacher, guide*, and *revelator*. He would also convict the world of *sin, righteousness and judgement*. The Holy Spirit is also known as the *Spirit of truth* and *He will guide us into all truth,* if we allow Him.

With all the information and disinformation available to us today, we need to know what is the truth. There is not anything hidden from The Holy Spirit. He is in the secret chambers of the wicked and is aware of all the things being done and plotted there. He searches and reveals all the hidden things of men's hearts and makes known the things Jesus wants to reveal.

The Promise Of The Holy Spirit

As Jesus prepared His disciples for when He was going to end His earthly work (ministry) and return to the Father, He began to teach them about The Holy Spirit and the purpose of The Holy Spirit. Like the Father, The Holy Spirit is invisible, but His presence and power are amazingly visible in the lives of those who believe and receive Him and those who give Him access to their lives. There are many in the 'Christian' world who are confused, ignorant, afraid, skeptical, etc. about the precious Holy Spirit, even though they cannot deny His existence and work in the early church. They struggle with Him being a major part of the health and wellbeing of the church and their supernatural lives today. However, everywhere He is welcomed and received, He brings the same gifts and glory He was tasked with to His church throughout the ages. He will continue to do so until Jesus returns to take His rightful place as Lord and ruler of the kingdoms of this world and all the earth.

[15] "If you love Me, keep My commandments. [16] And *I will pray the Father, and He will give you another Helper, that He may abide with you forever—* [17] *the Spirit of truth*, whom the world cannot receive, because it neither sees Him nor knows Him; but you know Him, for He dwells with you and will be in you. [18] I will not leave you orphans; I will come to you. John 14:15-18 NKJV

[5] "But now I go away to Him who sent Me, and none of you asks Me, 'Where are You going?' [6] But because I have said these things to you, sorrow has filled your heart. [7] Nevertheless I tell you the truth. *It is to your advantage that I go away; for if I do not go away, the Helper will not come to you; but if I depart, I will send Him to you.* [8] And when He has come, *He will*

convict the world of sin, and of *righteousness*, and of *judgment*: [9] of *sin*, because *they do not believe in Me*; [10] of *righteousness*, because *I go to My Father and you see Me no more*; [11] of *judgment*, because *the ruler of this world is judged.*[12] "I still have many things to say to you, but you cannot bear them now.[13] However, when He, *the Spirit of truth,* has come, *He will guide you into all truth; for He will not speak on His own authority,* but *whatever He hears He will speak;* and *He will tell you things to come.* [14] *He will glorify Me,* for *He will take of what is Mine and declare it to you.* [15] *All things that the Father has are Mine. Therefore I said that He will take of Mine and declare it to you.* John 16:5-15 BSB

The Work Of The Holy Spirit

The Holy Spirit came to do a work on the earth, even as the Lord had a work to do (John 17:4); which the Father gave Him. The Holy Spirit works in and through us in the following ways:

- ❖ He convicts us (and the world) of sin, righteousness, and judgement.
- ❖ He leads and guides us into all truth.
- ❖ He tells us of things to come.
- ❖ He glorifies Jesus by taking what belongs to Jesus and declaring it to us. He is subject to Jesus, since the Father has given everything to the Son. He does not speak on His own authority.
- ❖ He empowers the saints (church) to continue the kingdom mandate Jesus started, by giving supernatural gifts to the church.
- ❖ He helps us pray: *In the same way, the Spirit helps us in our weakness. We do not know what we ought to pray for, but the Spirit himself intercedes for us through wordless groans. Romans 8:26*
- ❖ He gives us the ability to live a life that is pleasing to God and those around us producing spiritual 'fruit' in us: *[22]But the fruit of the Spirit is love, joy, peace, patience, kindness, goodness, faithfulness, [23]gentleness, self-control; against such things there is no law. Galatians 5:22-23 BSB*

Baptism In The Holy Spirit And Fire

There is a difference between "having" The Holy Spirit, and being empowered for ministry by being baptized in The Holy Spirit and fire. This fact was evident in the life of the apostles, especially the apostle Peter. There was a stark and noticeable difference in his life and ministry after the Book of Acts 2. In Matthew 20:19-22, Jesus commissioned the disciples to the ministry and told them to receive The Holy Spirit, but it was only at the day of Pentecost this event took place. Many of us have received the "breath of the Lord" upon us, but we have never been fully immersed in the Holy Spirit, empowered and emboldened for ministry as in Acts 2. Therefore, our ministry (administering the affairs of God on the earth) is not as effective as it could be. People will argue that they "have The Holy Spirit", but there is very little evidence of The Holy Spirit having them. Their lives are powerless, shallow and dry. They are easily discouraged and overcome by fear and sin.

It is important to note that Jesus and John talked about two things: *Baptism of The Holy Spirit* and B*aptism of Fire*. Many of us "have" The Holy Spirit but have no fire. Some people might be very energetic, loud, demonstrative, emotional, etc. in the administration of their kingdom duties (preaching as they call it), but do not have the fire or anointing of the Holy Spirit to get the job done. I have experienced both The Holy Spirit and fire in my life, and I can tell you that having the fire, is another dimension of effectiveness in kingdom service (ministry). When you are touched by the fire of God, it electrifies you and everything you touch. Having the fire of God on our lives, requires a whole new level of consecration and holiness in our lives, and many of us are not ready for it. I desire both, and as previously stated have experienced both. However, the fire of God does not co-exist with compromise, sin, and lukewarmness, but it will only dwell in pure and holy vessels. *Let us make the pursuit of the supernatural gift of The Holy Spirit and fire, two of our major priorities,* as included in the riches of our glorious inheritance, in God's holy people.

> I indeed baptize you with water unto repentance, but He who is coming after me is mightier than I, whose sandals I am not worthy to carry. *He will baptize you with the Holy Spirit and fire.* Matthew 3:11 NKJV

> *God anointed* Jesus of Nazareth with *the Holy Spirit and with power,* who went about doing good and healing all who were oppressed by the devil, *for God was with Him* Acts 10:38 NKJV

> But *you shall receive power when the Holy Spirit has come upon you; and you shall be witnesses to Me* in Jerusalem, and in all Judea and Samaria, and to the end of the earth." Acts 1:8 NKJV

> [1] And it happened, while Apollos was at Corinth, that Paul, having passed through the upper regions, came to Ephesus.

> And finding some disciples [2] he said to them, *"Did you receive the Holy Spirit when you believed?"* So they said to him, "We have not so much as heard whether there is a Holy Spirit." [3] And he said to them, "Into what then were you baptized?"

> So they said, "Into John's baptism." [4] Then Paul said, "John indeed baptized with a baptism of repentance, saying to the people that they should believe on Him who would come after him, that is, on Christ Jesus." [5] When they heard this, they were baptized in the name of the Lord Jesus. [6] *And when Paul had laid hands on them, the Holy Spirit came upon them, and they spoke with tongues and prophesied.* [7] *Now the men were about twelve in all.* Acts 19:1-7 NKJV

> [44] While Peter was still speaking these words, the Holy Spirit

fell upon all those who heard the word. ⁴⁵ And those of the circumcision who believed were astonished, as many as came with Peter, because *the gift of the Holy Spirit had been poured out on the Gentiles also. ⁴⁶ For they heard them speak with tongues and magnify God.* Acts 10:44-46 NKJV

But you, dear friends, must build each other up in your most holy faith, *pray in the power of the Holy Spirit,* Jude 1:20 NLT

Receiving The Gift Of The Holy Spirit

The Holy Spirit is a good gift from the Father, not someone or something to be feared. Remember, every good and perfect gift comes from the Father of lights (James 1:17). If you desire the gift of The Holy Spirit, are born again of the Spirit of God, then you may receive Him a few different ways.

The first account of the "public" and magnificent outpouring of The Holy Spirit occurred on the Day of Pentecost *¹When the Day of Pentecost had fully come, they were all with one accord in one place. ²And suddenly there came a sound from heaven, as of a rushing mighty wind, and it filled the whole house where they were sitting. ³Then there appeared to them divided tongues, as of fire, and one sat upon each of them. ⁴And they were all filled with the Holy Spirit and began to speak with other tongues, as the Spirit gave them utterance.* Acts 2:1-4 NKJV

This event occurred as the result of the promise Jesus gave to His disciples, before He departed to heaven: *⁴And being assembled together with them, He commanded them not to depart from Jerusalem, but to wait for the Promise of the Father, "which," He said, "you have heard from Me; ⁵for John truly baptized with water, but you shall be baptized with the Holy Spirit not many days from* now." *⁶Therefore, when they had come together, they asked Him, say-ing, "Lord, will You at this time restore the kingdom to Israel?" ⁷And He said to them, "It is not for you to know times or seasons which the Father has put in His own authority. ⁸But you shall receive power when the Holy Spirit has come upon you; and you shall be witnesses to Me in Jerusalem, and in all Judea and Samaria, and to the end of the earth."* Acts 1:4-8 NKJV

During this event, you notice that no-one laid hands on the people in the upper room. The Holy Spirit came and filled every one of them and sat upon them like cloven tongues of fire. Wow!!!! What an amazing event. However, this was not a one time event. If you study church history, there were eyewitness accounts of this same type of outpouring happening throughout its history. The Azusa Street 'revival' was one of the most prolific in the last 100 years and its effects still reverberate around the world to this day.

Another way to receive Him, is to *ask the Father in heaven, for The Holy Spirit* (if you desire to have Him in your life). It is that simple, just ask Him. That is what I did when I learnt about the gift of The Holy Spirit, and how I could receive Him. I was first baptized in The Holy Spirit when I was water baptized, but did not understand what was happening, so I had to return with a better understanding and receive Him back into my life. Have the simple faith of a child and take the Lord at His Word. He is not a man that He should lie.

If you then, though you are evil, know how to give good gifts to your children, *how much more will your Father in heaven give The Holy Spirit to those who ask him*!" Luke 11:13 NIV

The most common way that people receive the baptism of The Holy Spirit, is by *having hands laid on them by another,* who has the gift of The Holy Spirit. This is the way I have helped many people receive the gift of The Holy Spirit. I have seen no difference in the receptivity between children and adults. I have seen both children and adults struggle to receive the gift of the Holy Spirit, and also seen both children and adults have no struggle receiving the gift. Sometimes, we have to get rid of so much religious baggage and fear before we can be open to what God desires to do in our lives.

[14]Now when the apostles who were at Jerusalem heard that Samaria had received the word of God, they sent Peter and John to them, [15]who, when they had come down, prayed for them that they might receive the Holy Spirit. [16]For as yet He had fallen upon none of them. They had only been baptized in the name of the Lord Jesus. *[17]Then they laid hands on them, and they received the Holy Spirit.* Acts 8:14-17 NKJV

[1]And it happened, while Apollos was at Corinth, that Paul, having passed through the upper regions, came to Ephesus. And finding some disciples [2]he said to them, *"Did you receive the Holy Spirit when you believed?"* So they said to him, "We have not so much as heard whether there is a Holy Spirit." [3]And he said to them, "Into what then were you baptized?" So they said, "Into John's baptism." [4]Then Paul said, "John indeed baptized with a baptism of repentance, saying to the people that they should believe on Him who would come after him, that is, on Christ Jesus." [5]When they heard this, they were baptized in the name of the Lord Jesus. *[6]And when Paul had laid hands on them, the Holy Spirit came upon them, and they spoke with tongues and prophesied. [7]Now the men were about twelve in all.* Acts 19:1-7 NKJV

Another way people have received The Holy Spirit is by the preaching of the Word of God. This happened when Peter preached Jesus to the Gentiles for the first time.

[44]While Peter was still speaking these words, the Holy Spirit came

down on all those who heard the message. ⁴⁵The circumcised believers who had come with Peter were astounded because the gift of the Holy Spirit had been poured out on the Gentiles also. ⁴⁶For they heard them speaking in other languages and declaring the greatness of God. Then Peter responded, " Acts 10:44-46 HSCB

I have seen this myself many times, where large groups of people were baptized in The Holy Spirit with the evidence of speaking in tongues, by hearing the Word of God about The Holy spirit, without hands being laid on them. It is all a matter of the heart. How open is yours to the message of The Holy Spirit and His purpose in the earth? I pray that your heart becomes wide open, so that it may be filled with the most beautiful gift after salvation, the precious Holy Spirit of God.

The Holy Spirit is also responsible for equipping/empowering the church to carry out its kingdom mandate, to destroy the works of the devil in the lives of God's children. He does so by giving supernatural gifts to us:

⁴*There are diversities of gifts, but the same Spirit.* ⁵There are differences of ministries, but the same Lord. ⁶And there are diversities of activities, but it is the same God who works all in all. ⁷ But the manifestation of the Spirit is given to each one for the profit of all: ⁸ for to one is given the *word of wisdom* through the Spirit, to another the *word of knowledge* through the same Spirit, ⁹ to another *faith* by the same Spirit, to another *gifts of healings* by the same Spirit, ¹⁰ to another the *working of miracles,* to another *prophecy,* to another *discerning of spirits*, to another *different kinds of tongues*, to another the *interpretation of tongues.* ¹¹ *But one and the same Spirit works all these things,* distributing to each one individually as He wills. Acts 12:4-11 NKJV

The study and understanding of The Holy Spirit and His purpose, is worthy of our time and energy. The Holy Spirit lifted off the face of the earth, after the fall of man. *Jesus had to die and return to heaven, for The Holy Spirit to be released back on the earth.* The work Jesus came to do on the earth was completed (it is finished). *The Holy Spirit, from the time He gave birth to the church, till Jesus returns will work on the earth with the sons of men to help them become the children of God. For all who are led by the Spirit of God are children of God. (Romans 8:14 NLT.)* This is the mystery that has been revealed to us through Jesus Christ, that we are the children of God, made in His image and in His likeness. The incredible and supernatural Holy Spirit, came to complete the work Jesus started. He came to equip (give supernatural gifts to) and empower all of God's children, so that they could live and operate as the children of God outside the realm of the natural.

FAITH: LIVING BY IT

Now faith is the substance of things hoped for, the evidence of things not seen. Hebrews 11:1 AKJV

W hat we profess to practice in our life (religious or otherwise), is often referred to as our system of Faith or Belief. This is true ast a basic level, because our system of beliefs drive our behavior. This makes what we base our faith on, doubly important. Anybody can have a good talk, but we are always most likely to tell what a person believes, by the way they conduct their lives.

At this point in the book, as believers in Jesus Christ, you should have a very clear understanding regarding the foundation of our Faith. Just in case you are wondering, I will sum it up the way I see it: *We believe in God the Father, His Son Jesus Christ, and The Holy Spirit. We believe that the three, are one. We believe that the only way to the Father, is through His Son Jesus Christ, who alone made a way for us to be reconciled to our creator and Heavenly Father. The way was made for us through the unjust execution (death) and powerful resurrection of Jesus. We believe His Word is divinely inspired, and reveals to us His will and His ways. We believe that The Holy Spirit is alive and active in the life of the church and every believer, who lives in obedience to the Father's words. We believe that Jesus is alive, seated at the right hand of the Father in heaven, and that at the time appointed by the Father is coming back again, to rule and reign on the earth as sovereign ruler and king. We will have rule and authority alongside*

Him on the new earth He is going to create.

Within our system of beliefs, there are many virtues that we adhere to or practice, e.g. hope, love, forgiveness, kindness, patience, etc. There is one virtue however, that was most often called out by the prophets, Jesus Himself and the apostles, other than love. *Faith.*

For in it *the righteousness of God is revealed from faith to faith*; as it is written, *"The just shall live by faith." Romans 1:17 NKJV*

And *it is impossible to please God without faith. Anyone who wants to come to him must believe that God exists* and that he *rewards those who sincerely seek him. Hebrews 11:6 NLT*

The Foundation Of Our Faith Is God.

Simply put, I like to think of faith *as believing, trusting Him and taking Him at His Word.* It is through hearing His Word, that we found out who Jesus was and what He came to do for us. It is through Jesus (The Living Word of God) that we came to know the Father and receive the Holy Spirit. *The Word of God instilled faith in us, and made us aware of the supernatural world that existed beyond our human sight.*

Then Jesus said to the disciples, *"Have faith in God.* I tell you the truth, you can say to this mountain, 'May you be lifted up and thrown into the sea,' and it will happen. *But you must really believe it will happen and have no doubt in your heart. Mark 11:22-23 NLT*

So then *faith comes by hearing, and hearing by the word of God. Romans 10:17 NKJV*

³By faith we understand that the worlds were framed by the word of God, so that *the things which are seen were not made of things which are visible. Hebrews 11:3 NKJV*

Faith is a force that can powerfully work in and through us, because the source of faith is God Himself. Faith is the connector or adapter that converts the power/word of God, into a form that can be utilized/consumed by mankind. *For indeed the gospel was preached to us as well as to them; but the word which they heard did not profit them, not being mixed with faith in those who heard it. Hebrews 4:2 NKJV.* The Word of God only becomes useful when we mix it with faith (trust and believe the source of the message).

The Promises And Power Of Faith

Jesus often taught on faith and some of the things He taught were mind blowing to His first disciples, and to most of us today. Some of the things He taught are so incredulous, that most teachers of God's Word, completely ignore it. Why is that? I know *when the Word of God is preached, a response is always required. God is not in the information sharing business, He is in the life trans-formation business.* His Word is profitable to us, for instruction, correction and reproof. If we teach these things as Jesus taught, we should expect to see them come to fruition. If we preach what Jesus preached, I believe people's faith will be stirred up to obtain these promises of faith, made in God's Word.

Let us look at some of the things Jesus taught and demonstrated about faith. Some may say that what Jesus taught was only symbolic, I agree to an extent, but some of those symbols were pretty big and ambitious (audacious).

22 So Jesus answered and said to them, *"Have faith in God.* 23For assuredly, I say to you, *whoever says to this mountain, 'Be removed and be cast into the sea,' and does not doubt in his heart, but believes that those things he says will be done, he will have whatever he says. 24Therefore I say to you, whatever things you ask when you pray, believe that you receive them, and you will have them.* Mark 11:22-24 NKJV

The Faith Connection

There are several instances where Jesus directly linked the person's faith in Him, as the reason why they received their miracle.

46 Now they came to Jericho. As He went out of Jericho with

His disciples and a great multitude, *blind Bartimaeus, the son of Timaeus, sat by the road begging.* [47]And when he heard that it was Jesus of Nazareth, *he began to cry out and say, "Jesus, Son of David, have mercy on me!"* [48]Then many warned him to be quiet; but *he cried out all the more, "Son of David, have mercy on me!"* [49]So Jesus stood still and commanded him to be called. Then they called the blind man, saying to him, "Be of good cheer. Rise, He is calling you." [50]And throwing aside his garment, he rose and came to Jesus. [51]*So Jesus answered and said to him, "What do you want Me to do for you?" The blind man said to Him, "Rabboni, that I may receive my sight."* [52]Then *Jesus said to him*, "Go your way; *your faith has made you well."* And *immediately he received his sight* and followed Jesus on the road. Mark 10:46-52 NKJV

[25]Now a certain woman had a flow of blood for twelve years, [26]and had suffered many things from many physicians. She had spent all that she had and was no better, but rather grew worse. [27]When she heard about Jesus, she came behind Him in the crowd and touched His garment. [28]For she said, "If only I may touch His clothes, I shall be made well." [29]Immediately the fountain of her blood was dried up, and she felt in her body that she was healed of the affliction. [30]And Jesus, immediately knowing in Himself that power had gone out of Him, turned around in the crowd and said, "Who touched My clothes?" [31]But His disciples said to Him, "You see the multitude thronging You, and You say, 'Who touched Me?' " [32]And He looked around to see her who had done this thing. [33]But the woman, fearing and trembling, knowing what had happened to her, came and fell down before Him

and told Him the whole truth. [34]And He said to her, *"Daughter, your faith has made you well. Go in peace, and be healed of your affliction." Mark 5:25-34 NKJV*

[21]Then Jesus went out from there and departed to the region of Tyre and Sidon. [22]And behold, a woman of Canaan came from that region and cried out to Him, saying, "Have mercy on me, O Lord, Son of David! My daughter is severely demon-possessed." [23]But He answered her not a word. And His disciples came and urged Him, saying, "Send her away, for she cries out after us." [24]But He answered and said, "I was not sent except to the lost sheep of the house of Israel." [25]Then she came and worshiped Him, saying, "Lord, help me!" [26]But He answered and said, "It is not good to take the children's bread and throw it to the little dogs." [27]And she said, "Yes, Lord, yet even the little dogs eat the crumbs which fall from their masters' table." *[28]Then Jesus answered and said to her, "O woman, great is your faith! Let it be to you as you desire." And her daughter was healed from that very hour.* Matthew 15:21-28 NKJV

There are many other instances where the Lord referenced the faith of the people who received miraculous/supernatural things from Him. Even though Jesus had the power and authority to heal, they needed a measure of faith and trust in His ability to do so.

There was a time when Jesus went to His own hometown and the people there had no faith in Him (they were over familiar with Him, and thought they already knew who He was). Although they acknowledged the things He did, they did not see any of God's power released to them because of their lack of faith.

[1]Then He went out from there and came to His own country, and His disciples followed Him. [2]And when the Sabbath had

come, He began to teach in the synagogue. *And many hearing Him were astonished, saying, "Where did this Man get these things? And what wisdom is this which is given to Him, that such mighty works are performed by His hands!* [3]*Is this not the carpenter, the Son of Mary, and brother of James, Joses, Judas, and Simon? And are not His sisters here with us?" So they were offended at Him.* [4]*But Jesus said to them, "A prophet is not without honor except in his own country, among his own relatives, and in his own house."* [5]*Now He could do no mighty work there, except that He laid His hands on a few sick people and healed them.* [6]*And He marveled because of their unbelief.* Then He went about the villages in a circuit, teaching. Mark 6:1-6 NKJV

Our faith (in God/Jesus) is a powerful way for us to connect and receive things which are beyond our natural eyesight. Jesus said it and that settles it for me. He has never been proven wrong.

Mustard Seed Faith

How do you know if you have enough faith, or how much faith you need for any given circumstance/situation in your life? I think Jesus understood that this question would be asked or at least be on people's minds. His answers to His disciples seem so simple. I have wrestled with it, and still do, with the answer Jesus gave His disciples.

[14]And when they had come to the multitude, a man came to Him, kneeling down to Him and saying, [15]"Lord, have mercy on my son, for he is an epileptic and suffers severely; for he often falls into the fire and often into the water. [16]So I brought him to Your disciples, but they could not cure him." [17]Then Jesus answered and said, "O faithless and perverse generation, how long shall I be with you? How long shall I bear with you? Bring him here to Me." [18]And Jesus rebuked the demon, and it came out of him; and the child was cured from that very hour. [19]Then the disciples came to Jesus privately and said, "Why could we not cast it out?" [20]So Jesus said to them, "Because of your unbelief; for assuredly, *I say to you, if you have faith as a mustard seed, you will say to this mountain, 'Move from here to there,' and it will move; and nothing will be impossible for you.* [21]However, this kind does not go out except by prayer and fasting." Matthew 17:14-21 NKJV

It is worth pursuing this answer Jesus gave us. Jesus said if we have faith as small as one of the smallest seeds in the world, we will be able to enter into this incredible world which is beyond our wildest dreams and what we deem possible. Jesus had this kind of faith and it seemed so natural for Him to have it. It was never a strain for Him to move in and out of the natural world and supernatural world. One minute, He is having dinner as a guest at someone's house and the next minute, in that same house, He raises a crippled man from his bed and gives him the ability to walk again. This is the kind of life He is inviting us into. Is it your desire to go there? I hope this is why you are reading this book. I certainly desire to go there and I will not stop having faith for it. I have tasted of this life and I desire much more of it. Since Jesus talked about prayer and fasting in the last scripture we looked at in this chapter, we will dive right into these two disciplines of our faith. Are you ready?

PRAYER

*Then Jesus told his disciples a parable to show them that **they** should always pray and not give up. Luke 18:1 NIV*

Prayer is powerful and beneficial, yet so neglected and over-looked as a discipline of the children of God. Our prayers are often done out of extreme need, distress, or desperation. Prayer, however, does not have to be so difficult or 'painful,' as we seem to think. Prayer should be a joy and a delight. It should be something we 'run' to with great anticipation. Prayer is thera-peutic and yields great dividends to all who do it on a regular and consistent basis. It is foundational to an effective and overcom-ing Christian life. Effective and fervent prayer open up more of the realm of the supernatural to us. It allows us to reach into the supernatural realm, and pull things into the natural realm. Prayer is also practiced universally in every religion and even some who do not believe in God or a god/deity, pray at times.

Effective And Fervent Prayer

There are key things that enhances our ability and the effectiveness of our prayer life.

- ❖ Effective prayer is *built on an intimate relationship with God.* This makes the commandment of knowing, understanding and loving God, of even greater importance.
- ❖ Effective and powerful prayer is *based on the Word of God*, therefore knowing God's Word is foundational.
- ❖ Effective and fervent prayer is *empowered by the Holy Spirit*, because we do not know at times how and what to pray, but The Holy Spirit helps us pray effectively and fervently.

Why Should I Pray?

It is strange for me to even ask this question since we live in a fallen world, where so much is out of our control and ability to change. Who has not prayed to something or someone at some point in life? Why should we pray?

- ❖ Prayer invites the participation of God in our lives, the lives of others, and in the affairs of nation and the world (see the Book of Esther).
- ❖ Prayer gives you spiritual power and strength for life (a prayerless life is a powerless life).
- ❖ Prayer keeps you out of temptation (gives you the power to overcome sin).
- ❖ Prayer brings peace and rest into our lives.

Jesus (Our Example) Prayed Often

³⁹Jesus went out as usual to the Mount of Olives, and his disciples followed him. ⁴⁰ On reaching the place, he said to them, "Pray that you will not fall into temptation." ⁴¹ He withdrew about a stone's throw beyond them, knelt down and prayed. Luke 22:39-40 NIV

As a believer in Jesus Christ, whom I have accepted as my Savior, Master and Lord; I strive to follow the example He set and the principles He taught in His Word. Praying is a discipline that Jesus completely embraced and demonstrated our need for. For us to do the things He did, we need to practice the things He did. He became like us to show us how to live a God-filled, overcoming and victorious life. Hebrews 2:17-18

Now it came to pass, as *He was praying in a certain place,* when He ceased, that one of His disciples said to Him, *"Lord, teach us to pray,* as John also taught his disciples." Luke 11:1 NKJV

[Jesus Prays on the Mount of Olives] *³⁹ Jesus went out as usual to the Mount of Olives,* and his disciples followed him. ⁴⁰ On reaching the place, he said to them, "Pray that you will not fall into temptation." ⁴¹ *He withdrew about a stone's throw beyond them, knelt down and prayed,* Luke 22:39 NIV

[Jesus Prays in a Solitary Place] Very early in the morning, while it was still dark, *Jesus* got up, *left the house and went off to a solitary place, where he prayed.* Mark 1:35 NIV

The results of the Lord's prayer life were so effective and apparent, that prayer was one of the few things the disciples ever asked Jesus to teach them (Luke 11:1).

Instructions To Pray

Watch and pray, lest you enter into temptation. The spirit indeed is willing, but the flesh is weak." Matthew 26:41 NKJV

The Bible has all the instructions for us to live a whole (holy), complete, effective, and overcoming life. Therefore, it contains all the instructions about why and how to pray. We do not need to invent new ways of praying, we just need to follow the principles and patterns of those who have gone before us.

So what shall I do? *I will pray with my spirit*, but *I will also pray with my understanding*; I will sing with my spirit, but I will also sing with my understanding. 1 Corinthians 14:15 NIV

[16] Rejoice always, [17] *pray without ceasing*, [18] *in everything give thanks*; for *this is the will of God in Christ Jesus for you.* 1 Thessalonians 5:16-18 NKJV

[Maintain Your Life With God] But you, beloved, building yourselves up on your most holy faith, *praying in the Holy Spirit* Jude 1:20 NKJV

How Do I Pray?

If consistent and effective prayer is new or a challenge, you might have to get someone to walk you through this process. Do not be afraid or ashamed to ask. Once you have learnt and mastered the art of praying, you will wonder how you ever lived without it. The rewards will be out of this world, so I implore and encourage you; master this discipline. Below are a few guidelines on how to pray:

❖ In everything, give thanks, for this is the will of God for your life. *First and foremost, give God thanks for His goodness and mercy towards you.* Thank Him for His many blessings. Thank Him for all the good things you have in your life (believe me, there are many good things, even when there are not so good things as well). Thank Him for His Word, Jesus, The Holy Spirit, the church.

❖ Pray in your understanding. Pray in your native language or another language you know and understand. I speak two natural languages fluently, and will often use one or the other too pray. It brings a freshness to my prayer life. I even know a little bit of Spanish, so I pray in the little I know sometimes as well.

❖ Pray in the Spirit if you have received that gift (see chapter on The Holy Spirit). If you have not yet received the gift of The Holy Spirit, find someone who has and ask that person to help you get to this point.

❖ Speak to your heavenly Father. Have a conversation with God. This might be awkward at first, but will become more natural with time.

❖ Pray the Word of God (His promises). Use God's Word when you pray. Remind God of His promises and His principles. Do not use vain repetitions (repeat the same phrase or words, over and over again).

❖ Do not pray to impress or be seen by others. Do not pray with flowery words (keep it real), it does not impress God.

❖ Prayer violently/strongly/fervently. Do not be timid. The devil loves timid Christians, he can intimidate them easily, but the fiery ones are not so easily influenced.

The Lord's Prayer Guidelines And The Model Prayer

[5] "And when you pray, you shall not be like the hypocrites. For they love to pray standing in the synagogues and on the corners of the streets, that they may be seen by men. Assuredly, I say to you, they have their reward. [6] But you, *when you pray, go into your room, and when you have shut your door, pray to your Father who is in the secret place; and your Father*

who sees in secret will reward you openly. [7] And when you pray, *do not use vain repetitions* as the heathen do. For they think that they will be heard for their many words. [8] "Therefore do not be like them. For your Father knows the things you have need of before you ask Him. [9] In this manner, therefore, pray: *Our Father in heaven, Hallowed be Your name.* [10] *Your kingdom come. Your will be done on earth as it is in heaven.* [11] *Give us this day our daily bread.* [12] *And forgive us our debts, as we forgive our debtors.* [13] *And do not lead us into temptation, but deliver us from the evil one. For Yours is the kingdom and the power and the glory forever. Amen.* Matthew 6:5-13 NKJV

Who And What Do I Pray For?

- ❖ Pray that His kingdom come and His will be done, here on earth, as it is in heaven.
- ❖ Pray for the spirit of wisdom and revelation that you may know Jesus better.
- ❖ Pray that the eyes of your understanding may be enlightened, that you may know what is the hope of His calling.
- ❖ Pray that you would know the riches of the glory of His inheritance in the saints.
- ❖ Pray that you would know what is the exceeding greatness of His power towards you who believe.
- ❖ Pray that you will be filled with the knowledge of His will.
- ❖ Pray for wisdom, knowledge, and understanding for the affairs of your life.
- ❖ Pray for yourself and your family, for God's protection, provision, guidance, etc.
- ❖ Pray for others in your church community, like you would pray for your family.
- ❖ Pray for the lost (family, friends, colleagues, etc.), that God would remove the blindness that the god of this world has placed over their hearts and minds, so the light of the gospel might shine into their lives.
- ❖ Pray for the church, pastors and leaders, that they would stay strong and faithful to God. Pray that they would be God pleasers and not people pleasers.
- ❖ Pray for your country and its leaders, that they would honor and respect God and His Laws.
- ❖ Pray for the world, for God so loved the world.

[15] Therefore I also, after I heard of your faith in the Lord Jesus and your love for all the saints, [16] *do not cease to give thanks for you, making mention of you in my prayers:* [17] that the God

of our Lord Jesus Christ, the Father of glory, *may give to you the spirit of wisdom and revelation in the knowledge of Him,* [18] *the eyes of your understanding being enlightened; that you may know what is the hope of His calling, what are the riches of the glory of His inheritance in the saints,* [19] *and what is the exceeding greatness of His power toward us who believe, according to the working of His mighty power* [20] which He worked in Christ when He raised Him from the dead and seated *Him* at His right hand in the heavenly *places,* [21] far above all principality and power and might and dominion, and every name that is named, not only in this age but also in that which is to come. [22] And He put all *things* under His feet, and gave Him *to be* head over all *things* to the church, [23] which is His body, the fullness of Him who fills all in all. Ephesians 1:15-22 NKJV

Confess *your* trespasses to one another, and *pray for one another*, that you may be healed. *The effective, fervent prayer of a righteous man avails much.* James 5:16 NKJV

praying always with all prayer and supplication in the Spirit, being watchful to this end with all perseverance and supplication for all the saints— Ephesians 6:18 NKJV

[*Preeminence of Christ*] For this reason we also, since the day we heard it, *do not cease to pray for you,* and to ask that you may be filled with the knowledge of His will in all wisdom and spiritual understanding; Colossians 1:9 NKJV

Likewise the Spirit also helps in our weaknesses. For we do not know what we should pray for as we ought, but *the Spirit Himself makes intercession for us with groanings which cannot be uttered.* Romans 8:26 NKJV

FASTING

If you hang around believers in Jesus Christ long enough, you will soon discovert that we love to feast. There is nothing like a great tender steak with some awesome seasoning and grilled vegetables. After that is done, you top it off with your most favorite dessert, and then a hot cappuccino or your beverage of choice. Eating makes us happy. Breaking bread (steaks) with other believers, has always been a way the church has maintained community and fellowship. However, the need to fast cannot be overemphasized.

Fasting is not unique to Christians. Buddhist, Hindus, Muslims, etc. all fast as part of their religious life. They all recognize the power of fasting, to solidify their commitment and devotion to their god/deity. Fasting however is God's idea and throughout the history of God's people, fasts were often embarked upon for various reasons. Esther fasted for the life of the nation of Israel. Ezra fasted during the rebuilding of Jerusalem. Many kings proclaimed fasts during their reigns. God honored their fast and intervened for them by bringing them supernatural victories over their enemies.

A couple of points to consider relating to fasting are the following: *Why do we fast? How do we fast? When do we fast?* The instructions and examples the Lord set, are the ones we should follow. Jesus did not start His earthly ministry until after He was baptized with The Holy Spirit and fasted forty days and forty nights. He led by example in all He taught. Remember, He said that a student is not greater than his master (but a student can be equal to his master). Whatever is demonstrated/required by/ of the teacher should/will be demonstrated/required by the student.

[1] Then Jesus was led up by the Spirit into the wilderness to be tempted by the devil. [2] And when *He had fasted forty days and forty nights, afterward He was hungry. Matthew 4:1-2 NKJV*

Why Do We Fast?

Humble yourselves before the Lord, and he will lift you up.
James 4:10 NIV

In view of the importance of food in the survival of all living beings, I believe that abstaining from it really says to God: *"I do not only need food for my survival, but I need You (God), as much as I need food."* Fasting brings humility, growth and maturity into the life of a believer as well. True humility says to God: *"I acknowledge my dependence and need for the life which You alone can give."* It says: *"You are the giver and sustainer of life."* True humility says: *"Every good and perfect gift comes from the Father of lights, in whom there is no variableness or shadow of turning."* True humility says: *"Whatever gifts, abilities, anointing I have, come from God and I will use them to bring glory and honor to His name; and not mine."* The humility gained through fasting, gets heaven's attention.

The primary reason for our fast, I believe, is to draw closer to God, so that God can be with us. It is when we are not so reliant on our own strength and abilities, that the supernatural life of God begins to flow through us in greater measure. We are supposed to reflect His image and His likeness, just as He intended us to do; when He originally created man. We are also supposed to continue the work Jesus started on the earth. *God anointed Jesus of Nazareth with the Holy Spirit and power, and how he went around doing good and healing all who were under the power of the devil, because God was with him. Acts 10:38 NIV*

Jesus taught on the importance and need for fasting in the lives of those who consider themselves His disciples.

²⁰ So Jesus said to them, "Because of your unbelief; for as-

suredly, I say to you, if you have faith as a mustard seed, you will say to this mountain, 'Move from here to there,' and it will move; and nothing will be impossible for you. *²¹ However, this kind does not go out except by prayer and fasting.*" Matthew 17:20-21 NKJV

³³They said to him, "John's disciples often fast and pray, and so do the disciples of the Pharisees, but yours go on eating and drinking." ³⁴Jesus answered, "Can you make the friends of the bridegroom fast while he is with them? *³⁵But the time will come when the bridegroom will be taken from them; in those days they will fast.*" Luke 5:33-35 NIV

The apostles went through severe times of testing and trials. They fasted often throughout their lives in Christ Jesus. From my own experiences with the discipline of fasting, I have found that it brings a tremendous sense of strength and peace, which is truly supernatural. I am almost always so much more energized in the supernatural, after extended periods of fasting.

How Do We Fast?

There a several accounts of how God's people fasted. The ones which are most often cited are the fasts of Esther, her hand-maidens, and the Jews in her province, when they were threatened with the extinction of their people. They fasted for three days, without food or anything to drink. Then, there is Daniel and the other captives from Jerusalem, who went to Babylon. They 'fasted' ten days without eating meats, delicacies, or drinking any wine. All they ate were vegetables and drank water. Jesus set a completely different standard. He fasted for forty days and nights. There are many other accounts of how God's people fasted throughout history.

This chapter is not meant to be an in-depth coverage on how to fast. There are many good resources in the market place to guide you through the process. Everyone should follow his own convictions and best judgement, based on his own personal situations. If you are in general good health, you should not have any problems fasting for periods of time. If your health is in question or if you have any misgivings, you should seek professional counsel before embarking on any type of fast.

Here are some general concepts and guidelines, when you are ready to embark on a period of fasting:

- ❖ Fasting does not 'change' God, it changes you.
- ❖ Do not see your fast as a way to get God to do something for you, see it as a way to get closer to Him and for your heart, mind and life to change.
- ❖ Do not fast to impress God or anyone else.
- ❖ Fasting should not be done to prove how spiritual or capable you are.
- ❖ If at all possible, keep your fast a private matter (except to those closest to you).
- ❖ Do not stop eating immediately when you start fasting.

Your body needs time to adapt to the reduction of calories, and cleanse itself.

❖ It is a good idea to cleanse your body first, this will prevent you from having headaches the first few days. One way to do this is by only eating fruits and vegetables for a couple of days, if you plan to not eat anything at some point during your fast. This depends on how long you intend to fast and what type of fast you are doing.

❖ Reduce the amount of food you are consuming gradually over a couple of days. Skip a meal or two or eat smaller meals.

❖ Drink plenty of water and other non-acidic, low sugar juices during your fast. Avoid caffeine.

❖ Use a mild laxative during your fasting to help keep your bowels moving. When you stop eating, your digestive track will go dormant causing irregular bowel movements, even though your bowels might still contain lots of matter. Do not overdo laxatives during this period.

❖   Do not go on an extended fast the very first time you decide to. I recommend a three-day fast, without consuming any solid foods, as a start This should be preceded by a cleansing period of at least three days, as mentioned earlier.

❖ As your discipline, will power and self-control increases, you can increase the length and type of fast you do. You can do seven, fourteen, twenty-one, or forty days of fasting. Do these with proper care and guidance. Never exceed a period of forty days.

❖ During your fast, you might be asked why you are not eating or may be invited out to eat. I normally tell people that I am not ready to eat, but that I will eat at a later time. At home, let your family know you will be fasting and for how long, and ask them not to share it with anyone outside the immediate family. It might be a good idea to stay out of the kitchen or restaurants during this time, depending on your self-discipline.

[16] *"Moreover, when you fast,* do not be like the hypocrites, with a sad countenance. For they disfigure their faces that they may appear to men to be fasting. Assuredly, I say to you, they have their reward. [17] *But you, when you fast, anoint your head and wash your face,* [18] *so that you do not appear to men to be fasting, but to your Father who is in the secret place; and your Father who sees in secret will reward you openly.* Matthew 6:16-18 NKJV

❖ Depending on how long you fast, you might lose a lot of weight. When people ask me about my weight loss, I usually tell them that I am in good health, and that it is a controlled and temporary situation. I let them know, I will be back to normal in a few weeks.

❖ Practice better hygiene than you usually do, during periods of fasting. During these times your body will be getting rid of many toxins and they are released through you pores, glands, digestive tract, etc. Buy plenty of sugar free and sweetener free mints to keep your breath fresh.

❖ Pray during your fast, it will keep you from breaking it before your intended time and will make your fast more impactful.

❖ Depending on your age and fitness level, you will be more tired than usual during the first couple of days of a fast. This normally happens when you stop eating solids foods. You might even get lightheaded at times. Refrain from doing any type of physical activities where you have to exert a lot of strength or energy. Rest more during these first couple of days. After a week or so, you will actually begin to feel stronger and have more energy.

❖ When you complete your fast, do not go on a binge eating spree. Believe me, your flesh would love to gorge itself on whatever it has been craving for during your fast. Pray and ask the Lord to help you not "pig out" when you break your fast. Gradually ease into your normal eating habits. If you have not eaten any meats or solids, do not eat them for at least as long as you have been fasting. Your body needs to gradually awaken and adjust to regular eating again.

When Do We Fast?

Fasting is more often done at an individual level but churches also fast corporately, once or twice a year. There were times, during ancient history, when the kings of Jewish nation would call for a national fast. Individuals, groups, and nations would often fast during periods leading up to and/or during extreme times of duress or national threats. I in my lifetime and in recent history, have never seen nations do a national fast.

However, since we are on a journey as believers in Jesus Christ, fasting should be a normal part of our lives. Jesus never compels or demands that anyone should fast. *Fasting is not a requirement for you to get God's approval, or for you to gain entrance to heaven.* Some religions fast to please their god/s, or to gain their approval. There is no such thing in our relationship with our living God.

The start of the new calendar year is always a good time to fast. It can be a good way to leave the previous year behind you and get yourself ready for the new year ahead. You can consider making this a regular time to fast, in your supernatural journey. I regularly join the fast my church does at the start of the new year after all the holiday parties have come to an end. It, however, is not the only time I fast during the year. I often go on more than one mission trip a year. I would normally prepare myself for these trips by fasting a few weeks before. This has become a regular part of my journey. I am not saying it is ever easy, but for me, it is necessary to prepare for the work we are going to be doing.

There are times I have felt prompted in my spirit to fast. Since I know that it is never my flesh that will prompt me to fast (I like eating way too much), I heeded this prompting most of the time. It is only after the fast, that I learn why I was prompted to fast. It normally is to get ready for a trial/test ahead, or for some attack of the enemy upon me or my family.

Outside of the 'whens' I just mentioned, you should consider fasting when you are facing hardships in your life: economic, emotional/relationship stress, mental or physical challenges in your life. Our battle is not against flesh and blood, but against unseen supernatural forces of darkness that come against us. Fasting gives us the strength to face and overcome these battles, by bringing God to our side to fight our battles for us. Master this discipline of fasting and you will see many supernatural victories in your life. They will become a common occurrence in your life, rather than an every once in a while event, like a solar or lunar eclipse.

LIVING THE GOD-PLEASING SUPERNATURAL LIFE

E verything we have covered up to this point, is to prepare and equip us to live God pleasing and impactful supernatural lives. You can live a supernatural life, without it being pleasing or acceptable to God. Jesus said this: *21"Not everyone who says to Me, 'Lord, Lord,' shall enter the kingdom of heaven, but he who does the will of My Father in heaven. 22Many will say to Me in that day, 'Lord, Lord, have we not prophesied in Your name, cast out demons in Your name, and done many wonders in Your name?' 23And then I will declare to them, 'I never knew you; depart from Me, you who practice lawlessness!' Matthew 7:21-23 NKJV*

This should be a sober warning to us to not lose focus on the things that the Lord is saying should be *the most important focus of our lives*: *doing the will of the Father and knowing Jesus*. Living the supernatural life is exciting and exhilarating, but not at the expense of being turned away from the kingdom of heaven, and the presence of the Lord. *If ever there were verses of scripture that we should have tattooed on our bodies, they should be these words Jesus spoke.* We should take His warning to heart and never forget it.

The Promise Of Living The Supernatural Life

The creator of everything made some incredible promises to His disciples and to everyone who believes in Him. Frankly, I am really astounded by these promises and endeavor to take Him at His word. I choose to believe every word and promise of His. Will you go on this journey with me? What do we have to lose?

> [12]*"Most assuredly, I say to you, he who believes in Me, the works that I do he will do also; and greater works than these he will do,* because I go to My Father. [13]And *whatever you ask in My name, that I will do, that the Father may be glorified in the Son. [14]If you ask anything in My name, I will do it.* John 14:12-14 NKJV

Jesus came not only to preach the supernatural/spiritual kingdom of God, but to effectively demonstrate it, through the works He did. He showed His mastery over the natural world by turning water into wine, multiplying five loaves of bread and two fish, and feeding five thousand men, besides women and children, with it. He cast out demons, walked on water, spoke to storms and made them stop, raised the dead, opened blind eyes and ears and knew things about people that no one ever revealed to Him (seeing into the unseen world), etc. These are the works He said we would do as those who believe in Him. *There is no founder of any other religion in the world,* to whom this can be credited. Then again, Jesus was not a religious leader and He did not come to start another religion. He is God in the flesh, who came to show us who we were meant to be and what we were meant to do.

My Journey Into The Supernatural World Of Jesus

I am naturally curious and like to discover, explore and experience different things. As a child, I loved to take my toys apart just to see how they worked. I could never put them back together again, probably to my mom's dismay. At age twenty-seven, I came to know Jesus for who He really is and it changed my life forever. The supernatural life of God began to flow into my life in such a way, that it was impossible to deny its existence. I had never experienced such love, grace and mercy before in my entire life.

When I started reading His Word, I was naturally curious and in awe of all the things revealed in it. I could not put it down for months. I read the second half of the Bible, from Matthew to Revelation, from cover to cover, a couple of times. I was like a child in a candy store, I could not believe what I read. It was absolutely amazing, exhilarating and beyond my wildest imagination. The things I read were better than any science fiction or action movie I had ever seen. Not only was it breathtaking to me, but I realized it was made available to me. I decided early in my journey of faith in Jesus Christ, that I was going to be a partaker of every promise and supernatural experience He made available to those who believed in Him.

Living In The Supernatural

Before I ever had anyone teach me anything, I started reaching into the supernatural world that Jesus talked about. Earlier I talked about me receiving the gift of The Holy Spirit, before I ever heard one sermon or teaching about Him. I desired to have Him, and I received Him very early in my life in Christ (I gave my life to the Lord in January and received the baptism of the Holy Spirit in April the same year, without anyone laying hands on me). I could not stop praying in tongues for about two weeks, it was all I desired to do. I still pray in tongues on a regular scheduled basis, at least four to five times a week. There are many times, as challenges come up in my life, that I pray in tongues as needed, outside of my regular scheduled prayer time. I was, and I am still, like a little child, receiving the kingdom of heaven, so that I can remain in it, after entering it.

You were meant to live beyond the natural. That was and is still God's intent. Jesus revealed and demonstrated everything the Father intended for His children to be and have. *We however, must do it God's way. This is a lifetime pursuit and you never get to a point in your life where you can stop and say; "I think I know it all now."*

The disciples were ordinary men and many of them were not formally educated, so they were often looked down upon by those who were educated. They were not scholars or teachers of the law, although they knew some of the law, traditions and words of the prophets. They had something that Jesus knew was required for them to continue the work He was starting on the earth. *They were going to trust and believe in Him and know that whatever they were going to accomplish, was going to be by His will and by His Power.* Jesus made this incredible promise to them, after He was raised from the dead:

but *you will receive power when the Holy Spirit has come upon you; and you shall be My witnesses* both in Jerusalem, and in all Judea and Samaria, and even to the remotest part of the earth." Acts 1:8 NASB

I am sure they did not fully comprehend what Jesus was saying (I would not have), but they trusted and believed what He was telling them. He was going to perform His Word, because He watches over His Word to perform it. On the Day of Pentecost, after His resurrection, Jesus fulfilled the promise He made to His disciples. There was a glorious outpouring of the Holy Spirit upon those who were in that upper room, waiting and praying, for the promise their Lord and Savior had made to them (Acts 2). The rest is history, as they say. The world has never been the same since the day those faithful servants of our Lord were launched into the supernatural world. They had only a few glimpses of it, up to that point.

> When they saw the boldness of Peter and John and realized that they were unschooled, ordinary men, *they marveled and took note that these men had been with Jesus. Acts 4:13 BSB*

Over the course of my life in Christ, I have had many glorious experiences in His presence. During some encounters I could not move or speak for hours. I have felt the presence of The Holy Spirit upon me so mightifully, many times, and still do. I have laid hands on the sick, and afflicted and have seen them healed and delivered. I have cast out demons. I have had words of wisdom and knowledge for people that were very accurate and life changing. All this happened in and through my life before I was given titles by man. This, however, did not happen in my life overnight. I've had many 'failures' over the course of my life. I have prayed for people who were sick and afflicted many times, and saw nothing happen. This did not deter me. I knew in whom I believed and that His Word was not going to return to Him void, it was going to accomplish that which He set it out to accomplish.

IN CONCLUSION

The supernatural Christ centered life is meant for all of God's children, without exception. It was never His intent that only a few of His "anointed" would function in this capacity. We are all the saints of God whom He desires to equip for the work of administering (ministry) His affairs on the earth: *[11]And He Himself gave some to be apostles, some prophets, some evangelists, and some pastors and teachers, [12]for the equipping of the saints for the work of ministry, for the edifying of the body of Christ, [13]till we all come to the unity of the faith and of the knowledge of the Son of God, to a perfect man, to the measure of the stature of the fullness of Christ; Ephesians 4:12-13 NKJV*

As I submitted myself to the five fold ministry gifts God placed in the church and started to walk the path I laid out in this book consistently, I began to walk in the supernatural on a regular basis. There are no shortcuts to pleasing God and walking in the promises He made to us. *Many desire to enter into this life, but there is a price to pay.* It is actually a very small price, in comparison to the rewards we receive in return. However, remember this: *God is much more interested in who we become, than in what we accomplish in His name.* My desire is that all of God's children receive a revelation of who He created them to be, and that all of us become empowered and activated for the mission He has given us:

[18]And Jesus came and spoke to them, saying, *"All authority*

has been given to Me in heaven and on earth. [19]Go therefore and make disciples of all the nations, baptizing them in the name of

the Father and of the Son and of the Holy Spirit, [20]teaching them to observe all things that I have commanded you; and lo, I am with you always, even to the end of the age." Amen. Matthew 28:18 NKJV

The ultimate purpose for us to live the Supernatural Christ-centered life, is to make Him known to the world.

Made in the USA
Columbia, SC
01 June 2020

98820238R00071